A GOLDEN DAWN

First edition. July 14, 2021.

Copyright © 2021 Terri Downes.

ISBN: 979-8215627716

Written by Terri Downes.

A Golden Dawn

Terri Downes

A Golden Dawn

Spring came late that year.

Mary could not help but worry a little as she stood outside on the lawn after Sunday hymn singing, shivering in the biting breeze. Surely by now it should have been warmer, she thought. She was concerned about what the late weather meant for the crops, although her father had told her not to worry.

"Worrying is just borrowing trouble," he would always say.

Mary knew that he was right, but knowing did not always help. She worried more than she should. She worried that the weather would never clear, and that the rain would rot the corn. She worried that the winter winds would damage the roof. She worried that her little sisters would catch colds.

She refused to call it worrying. She called it thinking, if anyone asked. "*I'm thinking.*"

Her mother always knew the truth.

"You think too much," she would say. And when she did not speak the words aloud, she would give Mary a look which said them for her.

She was giving Mary that look now.

Mary pretended that she could not see. She stared out at the gray horizon, running her finger absent-mindedly along her forearm, feeling the rise of an old scar beneath the fabric.

She tried not to look behind her, to where she knew Amos would be. She tried to think about the rain, and the corn, and colds, which were things that she could worry about, but not that she could control, so she would not have to do anything about them.

What was about to happen, however, was another matter entirely.

To some extent, this had not been in Mary's control, as it had been mostly arranged without her. She wondered if this was perhaps the reason, that her parents knew that she would think herself into dizziness if they had not simply presented the idea to her fully formed.

She was going courting.

Mary thought about the conversation her parents had had with her, only last week. They had broached the subject a number of times since she had turned sixteen, when the boys in the youth group had begun to take notice of her. It was natural that they should; Mary had blossomed into young womanhood more vividly than any other girl in the area. A number of the boys, with varying levels of confidence, had approached the subject of courtship, and had been turned down one by one.

Each time, Mary's parents had never asked her why she was not interested, only whether or not she was sure. After two years of this had passed, the invitations had lessened, and still there had been no comment. Several months after Mary had been baptized and started sitting with the married women at preaching every Sunday, Mary's mother had finally started to question her oldest child's reticence.

"Are you not just thinking about it too much?" she would ask.

Mary knew that she probably was, but she did not know how to stop herself.

"You could just give one a chance," her mother had suggested.

Mary had given it some thought – too much thought – and had not been able to decide on any one of the young men.

Whenever she started to consider one of them, she would immediately think of a reason why it would not work. One was too aloof, another too forward. Another was lazy. There was always a reason, and Mary could always imagine what might happen a few years down the road. So she continued to say no.

"Do you not want to wed?" her mother had finally asked.

This had been a month ago, while they were working together in the kitchen. Mary's mother had tried to make her question sound offhand, keeping her eyes focused on the pie crust she was rolling out. But she could not hide the worry from her voice.

"Of course I do," Mary had replied.

She tried to explain herself to her mother, who seemed to understand, although by the time Mary had finished she had rolled the pie crust into holes.

"So you do want to," she said again, as though to make doubly sure.

Mary assured her mother that she would love to be in charge of her own household, to have children and run a family.

But with whom? She had no idea.

So it had been something of a relief when her parents had approached her a week ago and told her that they had arranged for her to court Amos.

They had looked quite surprised when she had agreed without a single question. Mary guessed that they must have thought that she would start finding fault in Amos as she had with everyone else. But she knew her parents, and they knew her, and they would have made a good choice, she thought. At least she did not have to worry about it.

She did not know Amos. He had not been one of the boys from youth group to show an interest in her. In fact, she could not remember him ever showing an interest in anything.

Not that Amos was lazy. Mary knew that he worked on his family's farm, and occasionally went to help out at his cousin's farm a few miles away. But the one thing that she did know about Amos – the one thing that everybody knew about Amos – was that he was a dreamer.

Mary had glanced over at him this evening as she had arrived with her family. She had thought that he might be looking out for her, perhaps eager to share a smile at the thought of their planned ride home together afterward. But he was standing to the side with a group of young men, not even paying attention to what the group was saying. He had just been staring into the distance, as though having a completely different conversation in his head.

Mary had thought back to the little she had known of Amos when they were in youth group together. He had always done that, she had thought. She remembered hearing from his sisters that he was often in trouble at home – not through misbehavior, but simply forgetfulness. He seemed not to have grown out of it.

She had remembered, and wondered, and tried hard not to worry.

She was still trying.

The group from hymn singing had mostly cleared; it would be time for them to ride together soon. If Amos remembered, thought Mary. He seemed to be standing off to the side again, on the fringe of another group's conversation.

Her fingers strayed to her sleeve once more.

"Mary."

Mary turned to see her mother looking at her. She reached out and brushed an imaginary speck of dirt from her daughter's shoulder, then pulled the strings on her *kappe* straight.

"Stop thinking so much, child."

"I can't help thinking, *mamme*," said Mary, as she always did.

Mary's mother angled her body a little so she could share Mary's glance towards Amos.

"But if your head is full of what you think of him," said her mother, "how will there be space to learn what he is actually like?"

Mary blinked.

"Look at him," continued her mother. "You don't know him. Don't let your mind fill with thoughts that might not be true. You will find out what is real soon enough."

Mary nodded. She looked. As she did so, Amos turned and caught her eye. He seemed to come back to himself, and smiled.

Everyone else was heading to their buggies when he finally walked over and quietly asked if Mary was ready.

Mary was not sure she could answer that one way or the other, so she just smiled and walked with Amos to his buggy, sparing a single glance back over her shoulder to catch a final warning look from her mother.

As the buggy started off down the road, Mary wondered how other people managed to stop themselves from thinking.

Look at him, Mary's mother had said. The sun was almost gone, but she had a better chance to look at Amos now than she ever had before.

He had the same dark gold hair as the rest of his family, curling at his ears and forehead. His skin was tan, even now, as they made their way out of winter. Light gold. In fact, with his bright, tawny-oak eyes, he seemed gold all over, shining slightly through the gloom of the evening.

He glanced over, and Mary realized she was staring. She quickly turned and looked out of the window, her head filling with concerns that he might think her impolite.

Before the thoughts could take root, however, Amos interrupted them.

"I see the bad weather hasn't deterred the daffodils."

He gestured out to the low bank running alongside the road. It was starred with pale flowers coming up in clumps.

Mary felt her spirits sinking a little. Were they to discuss flowers, now? Was the whole ride to be taken up with polite small talk on subjects Amos guessed she would be interested in?

"I'm glad to see them brightening up the place," she offered.

"I'm not."

Mary paused, confused.

"Why?"

"One of our horses – not this one, the one with the dark mane, you know?"

"Pepper?" Mary dredged the name up out of her memory.

"Yes, Pepper – as of a week ago, he has developed a sudden and passionate urge to eat them."

"To eat... the daffodils?"

"Yes." Amos shook his head. "Just out of nowhere. Every time we take him out, he lunges for them like they're his private horse version of manna. And he gets very offended when we won't let him take a bite."

"Aren't daffodils poisonous?"

"Yes! They are. I have tried to explain this to Pepper, but do you think he listens?"

Amos gave an exaggerated sigh and scowled at the innocent faces of the daffodils they passed.

"I've often found it difficult to get horses to listen to reason," said Mary, keeping a straight face.

"I wanted to borrow him this evening, but I thought he might drag us to the bottom of a field somewhere in search of daffodil snacks. I would have had to pull the buggy back myself."

The visual made Mary laugh aloud. Amos turned a little and grinned at her.

"It's good to see you relaxing a little."

Mary blushed. So he had noticed her tension beforehand. Perhaps this observation should have made her tense once more, but Amos' open expression and friendliness prevented it.

"I don't often do this," she said.

"I know."

Mary immediately worried that he would ask her why, but he did not, allowing a quiet moment to pass.

"I think we all want things that are bad for us," he observed. "At some time or other."

"It's a good test of our character," said Mary. "Although I must say I've never been tempted to eat the local plant life."

Amos laughed.

"No doubt Pepper will have grown immensely in his character by the time the season is over. He'll be the wisest horse for miles."

"I'm sure."

Another moment of silence turned itself over.

"Which do you think is more difficult," asked Mary suddenly, surprising herself, "to want something that's bad for you, or not to want something that would be good for you?"

Amos thought about this for a minute.

"I suppose the second one," he said. "It might be harder to make yourself do something than to stop yourself from doing something. You have to take action instead of staying still."

Mary nodded.

"But it can be just as rewarding," Amos said, and then paused. "I'm glad you agreed to this, Mary."

Mary smiled, enjoying the warmth that comes from being understood.

She smiled again when he asked her if they could ride together the following week, and again when her parents had asked her how it went. She went to bed smiling, for the first time since she could not remember when.

They rode together the next week, and the week after. Amos would come over for his brief visits on Saturday, and for long, lingering talks on Sunday evenings.

The morning after their first ride together, Mary had immediately plunged into worry over the difficulties of getting to know a person from scratch. How long would it take to feel safe enough with someone before you consider spending your life with them?

Sure, their conversation the evening before had gone well, but there would be so much more for each of them to share. How on earth could they get to all of it?

But when she was with Amos, he never gave her a chance to start worrying. He seemed to immediately sense when her head was too full of thoughts, and he would chase them away with a funny story or stray observation.

And when she was troubled and knotted up, he would tell her stories. Long, winding tales that ebbed and flowed and caught every thought in their path. Each sentence would draw Mary away from the threads of worry, serving as a gentle rebuke for letting herself get knotted in the first place.

"What do you think happens next?" he would ask when he got to a bend in the tale, and would not continue until Mary had guessed.

She wondered how he managed to sense her moods. He did not seem to pay enough attention to anything to have developed such keen observational skills.

Now that she was trying to know him better, Mary tried to gauge Amos' interactions with others when she saw him at preaching or hymn singing. His reputation as a dreamer was certainly well earned. He would often lose the thread of a conversation entirely, drifting off and staring at nothing, until someone called his attention.

He then would normally apologize, laugh, and make a self-deprecating comment at which everyone could chuckle.

Perhaps he tried harder when they were together, Mary thought. Or maybe he found it easier to focus on one person at a time. But even though his eyes would drift away sometimes, he himself would remain present.

Mary did wonder, in the first couple of weeks, just how much attention he was paying when she was the one speaking. On the third Sunday evening they spent together, an hour or so into the conversation, she noticed him staring into the fire. She had been recounting a story from earlier in the week. Her little sister Elsa, the second youngest at eight years old, had tried to see if she could fit into an empty barrel in the barn. She had become stuck, and had then been too embarrassed to call for help. The rest of the family had spent over two hours searching for her before Mary had found her wedged into the barrel. It had then taken another fifteen minutes to get her out without risking splinters.

Mary was about halfway through the tale when she was suddenly seized with the conviction that Amos had not been listening at all, and that if she were to stop speaking he would not even notice. So she did.

Amos turned towards her within seconds, his expression confused.

"So where did you find her?" he asked.

Mary paused, irritated with herself for letting her thoughts get the best of her again.

"Wait, you did find her, right? She's not still out there somewhere?" Amos raised an eyebrow in mock concern.

Mary hesitated. "I'm waiting for you to guess what happens next," she said.

She wondered, afterward, what he would have thought if she had told him she was trying to make sure he was paying attention.

Surely people must do this all the time to him, she thought. *He is always staring off at nothing. This must be normal. He should not be offended by someone making sure.*

But something had held her back. Perhaps this was part of getting to know him, Mary thought.

Two weeks after that, he left without his coat. He returned for it twenty minutes later. Mary had seen it as soon as he had left, and was already waiting with it on the porch.

"I thought you might need this," she said, holding it out to him as he walked up the steps.

He stopped one step below her and took the coat, ducking his head a little as he blushed.

"Sorry."

"It's all right," said Mary.

"I think," said Amos, as he shrugged on the coat, " the problem is that I want it to be summer so badly that my mind's started to pretend I don't need a coat. Wishful thinking."

"Just so long as your mind doesn't convince you to try harvesting a green field," warned Mary.

Amos chuckled, his eyes golden in the light of the porch lamp as he looked up at her.

After he had left – for the second time – Mary went back inside. Her father met her as she walked through the door.

"He remembered before he got home, then," he said, shaking his head. "His father was just the same, when we were young. He grew out of it, though."

"Oh?" Mary supposed this was why her father had suggested Amos. He would not have done so if he had thought he would remain so absent-minded.

"*Jah*. And it was never that bad, I suppose. He never... caused any real problems."

Mary nodded. As she walked to the kitchen, she raised her right hand to her left forearm in an old, familiar gesture. She ran her fingertips slowly up the length of her scar, feeling each bump and furrow in the thickened skin.

She was sure that her father had been thinking of this when he spoke to her.

She could not bring it up, though. It would make him so sad.

It had been years ago, when Mary was only six. Her father's grandfather – Mary's great grandfather – had been staying with them since his wife had passed.

Mary had not realized how old he was, thinking him to be a similar age to her grandparents. But although his intelligence and wit were strong, he would forget things. Small things, at first. Where he had left something, what time it was. Then he started getting lost. He would walk off and disappear, and the boys would have to stop work to search for him.

He would always be embarrassed about it. He knew that he was forgetting things, and he hated it, but he could not do anything to stop it.

The accident had happened one morning in early fall. Mary had been working with her mother in the kitchen when her great grandfather had walked in, obviously having one of his far-away moments. He had not responded to her mother's greeting, but had wandered toward the stove. Seeing a pan of potatoes about to boil over, he had reached out to move it, forgetting to use a cloth. When the long metal handle burned his hand, he pulled away with a jerk, knocking the entire pan over and onto Mary, who had been coming over to move the pan herself.

Mary did not remember exactly what happened after that. She thought she could remember someone screaming, though she wasn't sure if it had been herself or her mother. She remembered the confusing brightness of the *Englisch* hospital, and the thickness of the bandages on her arm.

She remembered crying when the bandages had come off – not from pain, but from the shock of seeing her skin like that, like melted wax. The scar ran the length of her forearm, widening from a point on the back of her wrist as it moved up to envelop her elbow.

While he still lived, Mary's great grandfather had always had trouble speaking to her after that day. His gaze would trip over her, trying to land anywhere but her arm, anywhere that would not be a reminder of his fault.

Despite the forgiveness she had given – and given again and again when resentment had crept up on her – Mary had never been able to think of anything to say to him that would make things better.

Her mother had told her, years later, how her great grandfather had asked for help after that, trying to swallow his pride, and how he had so clearly hated every nudge and reminder. She did not want Amos to every feel that way – especially if he did not need to.

So she did not mention it when he was late, and tried not to mind. At least he remembered to come, and was always apologetic when necessary. She did not suggest that he leave a note for himself somewhere, or tie a knot in his handkerchief, even though she wondered daily whether such measures would help at all.

Amos seemed not to mind the lapses himself, always being ready with a joke afterward. And nothing that bad had ever happened. Mary did not want to overstep her boundaries and make him feel as though there was something wrong with him, that he needed looking after.

It would not be worth it to upset him, to have have that golden smile dimmed when she had started looking forward to it so much every week.

Thing continued along in this way for a while. The days began to lengthen and grow warmer. People's talk turned to crops, and estimating harvests. Mary's father and brothers were kept busy planting, the late arrival of spring giving them less time than they would normally have had to complete the task.

Amos spent most of each week with his cousin, who was similarly in need of extra work – his five older brothers meant that he could be spared from his own family's farm. He was full of stories about his cousin's family every Sunday, keeping Mary laughing for hours at a time.

After a while, she began to wonder why he had not yet brought up marriage. They were obviously getting on very well, and things were clearly headed in that direction, but the subject remained untouched.

In an uncharitable moment, Mary wondered if Amos had simply forgotten to ask her.

She tried not to worry about it, but as the weeks started adding up, the concerns became harder to put aside. He would need to ask her soon, so they could prepare to be married after harvest. Surely he did not mean to wait a whole year until next fall?

The answer came along with the summer. Mary often wondered, afterward, if the story would have ended differently if things had not happened the way they did.

It was a low, sultry day, warmth having finally arrived but failed to draw away the clouds. The world looked strange with the sky so dark and heavy, almost as though it were winter all over again.

Mary and Amos had been riding in the buggy for almost an hour. Amos had been telling another story, trying to get Mary's thoughts away from the possibility of a storm. She knew that thinking about the dangers was useless. It was not as though her worries could be used as a covering for the fields to spare them from damage.

So she tried to keep looking at Amos, and not out at the threatening weather. His skin had deepened in shade in the brief span of good weather they had had, and his hair was beginning to lighten. He seemed more golden than ever.

Just what everyone needs on such a dark day, Mary reflected. Their own private sun.

Thinking about this, she finally turned and looked out at the landscape, focusing on the fields and hedgerows instead of the clouds.

The unfamiliar fields and hedgerows.

Her eyebrows pulled together as she tried to make sense of what she could see. The shape of the hills ahead looked a little familiar... but the cluster of trees over to her right was not one she knew, Mary was sure. Yes, there was a stream running over to the left of them, she would recognize that if she had ever seen it before.

"What's the matter?" asked Amos.

"I'm not sure where we are," said Mary. "What turning did you take after the Miller's farm?"

When Amos did not answer right away, Mary felt her heart begin to sink.

"I'm not sure," he said eventually. "I'm afraid I wasn't paying attention."

He reigned in the horse a little, to a slow walk.

"Are you going to turn around?" asked Mary, keeping her tone as unconcerned as she could. "Or keep going until we find our way back?"

"I think... maybe turn around, that seems safest," said Amos, as Mary had hoped he would.

She nodded in relief, and kept quiet as he turned the buggy to go back the way they had come.

She expected him to make a joke or comment, but he did not. In fact, he remained quite quiet for several minutes.

Taking her cue from the way Amos usually managed to soothe her nerves, Mary began talking of her mother's plans for canning in the upcoming months, trying to keep the atmosphere light.

It was not until another half hour had passed that they had to face the inevitable.

"I still don't know where we are," said Mary, hoping against hope that Amos would laugh at her and point out a nearby landmark that was both familiar and obvious.

He did not.

"Neither do I. I think we must have gone down a side lane before coming onto this road. Perhaps one of the lanes leading off that way." He indicated to their left.

"I wish we had bigger hills in this area, or even mountains," Mary commented. "It would be much easier for navigation."

"I bet it would," said Amos absently.

The first lane led to a gate which they had definitely not gone through earlier. Amos turned the buggy again and they headed back once more. It was not until they tried the third turning that they recognized the way.

By that time, what little daylight had been allowed through the clouds was already draining away. Amos put the buggy's lights on without comment.

Mary tried to calculate what time they would get home, and whether they would manage it before her parents started worrying in earnest. Her hands began working at the corner of her apron, folding it into little pleats.

"I'm sorry," Amos said, looking at her expression. His voice was quieter than usual.

"It wasn't your fault," said Mary. "Relax."

"I can't," he said. "I shouldn't."

"What do you mean?"

"I can't relax, this is exactly what happens when I relax."

"...You get lost?"

"I *forget* things. I forget the time, I forget to pay attention. I try so hard to remember everything, but sometimes it's like my mind is water. I mean... well, you know."

"I know," Mary said, unable to deny it.

Amos glanced at her through the gloom which had begun to settle around them, and his expression was pained.

"I know everyone finds it funny, or annoying, but they have no idea how many things I would forget if I wasn't always trying so hard."

"Well, it's only little things," said Mary. "If you're a bit late here and there, what does it matter?"

"No, it's not just little things." Amos took a deep breath, as though to make a confession. "I've lost the horses before – forgot to lock them up, and they wandered away in the night."

"That's not so – "

"Not only once, either. Four different times, I did that. I've missed Sunday preaching before, just from forgetting what day it was. And you know I've been going down to help my cousin at his farm? My mother asked me to take some canning jars along for his wife. The box has been sitting there for three weeks, and every single morning I forget to take it with me."

Mary considered this.

"Couldn't you leave a note for yourself? Or put them by the door, the night before?"

"I shouldn't have to. No-one else has to," said Amos, his tone one of resentment.

"Someone could remind you," said Mary.

I could remind you, she thought. *If we were married.*

"They shouldn't have to," he insisted. "Why should I burden someone else with taking care of me, as though I were a child?"

"Perhaps they wouldn't mind," suggested Mary. *If they loved you.*

"They would," Amos said flatly. "Maybe not at first, but they would grow tired of it. Trust me."

It seemed almost as though Amos was desperate to explain, to have Mary feel the same way he did. As though he needed her to understand – and she did. Finally, she understood. This was why he had not asked her to marry him. He had known of his problems, and he wanted to get control over them before he tried to take charge of a household.

But he did not have control, she could see that plainly.

"You've... well, you've never hurt anyone," she said.

When Amos closed his eyes for a moment, she knew what was coming.

"Last year," he said, "I left the barn door open and forgot about it. The wind blew it shut onto my little brother's hand. He broke two fingers."

Mary remembered seeing little Karl with bandages on his hand last winter. She had assumed it had been done playing.

Her fingers reached up automatically, resting on her scar.

And she was angry. She could not be angry with Amos for forgetting things, for something he could not help. She saw now that she had been right, that he really did mind it that people saw how much he struggled, and that he tried to make the best of things.

She was angry that he had begun this courtship without knowing how it would end, without knowing if he could ever ask her to marry him. Had he thought she would just wait around for him to suddenly change the way his mind worked?

Would he have married her without knowing whether he could handle the responsibility of a family? Would he have done that, knowing that it could be his own children suffering from his forgetfulness in the future? Her children, with fingers broken in barn doors?

And he did not want to burden her with helping him, he seemed to be saying. She would just have to sit by and pray that he did nothing to harm their family.

She held her arm out, turning it a little so her scar was completely visible from end to end beneath the hemline of her elbow-length sleeve. Shadows sank into every crevice, the pale light catching every twist and line in the rough skin.

"Do you know how this happened?" Mary asked.

Amos looked a little thrown at the sudden change of subject, but he shook his head.

"An accident at home, I think you said?"

"I never told you the story, then."

Amos shook his head once more.

Mary told him.

She could not look at him, as she spoke, knowing what this would do to him.

He did not say anything. He did not need to. Mary could see that he understood exactly what she meant by telling him this story. She did not mention him once, never drawing a comparison between his story and hers. But he understood, and he remained silent.

The silence stretched on – not comfortable and spacious, as it had been so many times. It was heavy, stiff, holding each of them in place, sealing their jaws shut.

When they arrived at Mary's home, Amos managed to pull off his usual friendly manner. He apologized to Mary's parents for their lateness, and explained what had happened. He even managed to get her father to laugh when he said they had been ready to send for help using smoke signals.

He said goodbye politely. Mary nodded and wished him a safe journey home. Neither of them mentioned seeing each other again.

As Mary settled herself by the fireside to finish her day's mending, she felt her mother's worried gaze from across the room. She kept her head down, staring at her needle as though it might disappear without proper observation. She knew that if she looked up, her mother would take the opening and start asking questions.

She let her thoughts remain on Amos, on her disappointment and frustration. As odd as it was, she wanted to keep those thoughts present in her mind for as long as possible. She knew that once they faded, she would be left only with sadness.

By the time she went to bed, the process had already begun. Mary lay awake next to little Elsa, lying flat on her back and staring up. Her fingers worked at the edge of the sheet, pleating and folding it the way she did to her apron when she was nervous. Her anger betrayed her by melting away, and she was left thinking about how quiet Amos had been as she had told him the story.

Too many thoughts. They whirred around her like moths, fluttering against the edges of her mind, keeping her awake.

She wished that this had happened sooner, before she had grown to know Amos so well. Then she wouldn't have known how badly he'd been hurt.

No, she wished that she had never agreed to this courting in the first place.

She closed her eyes for a moment, imagining that.

Then she opened them and took the wish back.

No, she would not wish away the time she had spent with Amos. Even with all this trouble, she could not wish away the stories and the silences and the laughter.

And what does that mean? Mary wondered. Did it mean that marrying Amos would make any trouble worth it?

And it would be trouble, Mary thought. It would be a lot of work, making sure that Amos did not drift away from his duties, that everything was kept safe and running smoothly. Not so much work as he had seemed to think – not so much as taking care of a child, she knew that from caring for her two sisters and three brothers as they had grown up. But she would need to always think ahead, checking in with Amos constantly. And once they did have children, it would be even more work. There would be risk.

As Mary lay still, staring up into the darkness above, she finally asked herself: would that make it impossible? Or just... hard? Could she commit to this in the same way she would commit to having children, or to making breakfast every morning?

She knew, now, what she would be agreeing to. It would be an informed decision. But, Mary reasoned, if Amos were to become hurt in some way after they had been married – God forbid – she would be willing to care for him. Even if he were bedridden. And this would not be nearly so difficult.

The problem, really, she thought, smoothing the crimped edge of her sheet back down, was whether or not Amos would be willing to let her help.

Was he really just worried that she would not be able to love and respect him if she had to help him in this way? Or was he too proud to accept the help in the first place?

That was not something that Mary could answer.

She sat up. No, she could not answer that – only Amos could.

Mary slid quietly out of bed, careful not to wake Elsa. She felt carefully for her clothes, picking them up and carrying them with her downstairs. Glancing at the clock in the hall, she saw that it was only half an hour past three – she had thought it was later.

No matter, she decided, as she dressed in the kitchen. She would make the time pass.

It was the earliest she had ever started on her morning chores, but it felt good to work and clear her head. She laid the wood and kindling in the stove, ready to be lit, then set the breakfast things out, ready to be used when everyone came downstairs. She swept the kitchen floor – and then took a candle and swept the hall, being as quiet as she could. She knew she was probably doing a bad job in the wavering half light, but this was more for her own sake than necessity's.

She had just finished a completely unnecessary scrubbing of the counter tops when her mother came into the kitchen, a bemused expression on her face.

"Did the sun forget to rise this morning?" her mother asked, a smile tugging at the corner of her mouth, "or have you forgotten how to tell the time?"

"I couldn't sleep, *mamme*."

"Hmm."

Mary's mother walked past her and busied herself lighting the stove.

"What time is it?" asked Mary, realizing that she had not checked the clock since sweeping the hall, suddenly worried that she had left it too late.

"Five o'clock. Why?"

"I... have to run an errand," said Mary, grabbing her shawl. "Is that all right?"

"Is this anything to do with why you looked so miserable last night?" asked her mother.

Mary nodded hesitantly. Her mother smiled at her.

"Don't be too long," she said.

When Mary slipped out of the kitchen door, the sky was just beginning to lighten. Yesterday's clouds had blown away in the night, and the sky stretched high and colorless above her.

Amos had told her he normally left home at half past five every morning in order to get to his cousin's farm by the time the work started. And his home was a little over a mile away... yes, there was time.

She heard Amos' voice in her head, asking: *what happens next?*

As she walked, rather than batting away worries that flew around her head, Mary made plans. How to help someone remember to close a door, she wondered. Perhaps a mark in the door frame, at eye level, as a reminder. Or perhaps the person could do something every time they closed the door. Like tap it twice, or say a word to themselves, to help solidify the memory of closing it.

And remembering what work needed to be done – well, why not a list? It could be written out every morning, and have every item crossed off when the job was completed, just like Mary had used to do with her school tasks.

We could try a few different things, Mary decided. *And see what works.*

...If he is willing.

Even sooner than she had thought, Mary found herself at Amos' family home. She hoped that she had timed this correctly. She did not want to have to knock on the door, that would definitely embarrass Amos.

It should be about the right time, she thought, noting light at the kitchen window. If he is not late...

Mary heard a door open and close, and recognized Amos through the dim light as he walked down the path. She stepped out toward him. He stopped dead, and Mary took a moment to enjoy his slightly stunned expression.

He opened his mouth, but Mary spoke first.

"The jars."

"Uh... sorry?"

"You need to take the jars, for your cousin's wife."

Amos glanced down at his hands as though expecting to see a box of jars suddenly appear. Then he looked back up at Mary and gave his head a short, sharp shake, like he was not sure whether he had really woken up yet.

He spoke slowly. "You're here to..."

"To remind you to take the jars. The poor woman's been waiting for three weeks, Amos," said Mary.

She spoke breezily, but studied his face as she did so, watching carefully for signs that he would be angry. If he was, she knew that she would have to just let things be. Go home and tell her parents that it was not going to happen.

What happens next?

He did not look angry. A little sheepish, perhaps.

"Thank you," he said.

Mary tipped her head to the side.

"No, really, thank you." Amos nodded earnestly. "For going to the trouble."

"No trouble," said Mary.

Amos raised an eyebrow.

"Well, yes, it was," admitted Mary. "But it was a trouble I was willing to take. That I wanted to take. I want to help."

"Really," said Amos.

He still did not look offended, Mary thought, relieved. Though he did look doubtful. She tried to explain.

"Yes... I've been coming up with ideas. I think they'll work – I think that I can help you. If you let me."

Amos looked at her for a long moment, until Mary began to wonder whether was

going to say anything at all. Then he swallowed, glancing up to the sky for a moment before speaking.

"...And you really think you could do this, and not grow tired of it?"

Mary took a deep breath.

"Some work is more rewarding than others," she said.

Amos smiled at her, his broadest smile, the edges of his eyes creasing. Mary found herself smiling back. She felt as though she were watching a sunrise, light diminishing the shadow inch by inch.

"Although you could make it easier," she could not help adding.

Amos blinked a little.

"What do you mean?"

"I mean if we were married, I wouldn't have had half an hour's walk to remind you about the jars."

Amos laughed, then. And everything was golden.

Finally Amish

26

Erica Fanning

"There are some instances when it's good to be single. In the Plain community, when you're a teacher, being single is for the best. You can devote all of your time to teaching the community's children since you don't have any of your own."

Ruth was sure Mr. Troyer meant well, but he was a little old-fashioned for most people's liking and too blunt for anyone's taste. Ruth had been the only person in the entire community that actually tolerated him... and on occasion she had been given some really great advice.

This one-sided conversation was a great example. As Mr. Troyer went on about the pros of being a single woman in the Plain community, Ruth finally realized that must be her calling. That was what the Lord wanted her to do. She noticed that Mr. Troyer had finished talking and was staring at her. She apologized and explained to him what she had been thinking. He smiled, bringing the whiskers at the end of his mouth up about a half inch.

"I always knew I liked you, Ruth Miller. You're always using that beautiful mind that God gave you." He shuffled out of the store proudly. Ruth had just made his day, and it caused her to smile.

As she returned to work, she thought about the reason she was still single. She never wanted this life, but she didn't want to go through the entire courting process again just to be heartbroken. Her parents were extremely gracious and allowed her to work in their market and help care for the younger siblings since she wasn't ready to be a teacher at the time.

That was ten years ago, and she felt it was time to move on to being a teacher. The current teacher had retired at the end of the school year and so far, no one had stepped up to take the position. Ruth still needed to talk to her parents about leaving the family business, but she knew her brother Isaac would be taking over the entire business since he already had a son to pass everything onto in the future.

Suddenly Ruth's sister Mary came running from the back of the store. "Ruthy!" She seemed almost unable to contain whatever excitement she had. "Did you hear the news?" Ruth stopped what she rearranging the apples for the fifth time to give her youngest sister her fullest attention. Mary's entrance was the most exciting thing to happen today; the apples could wait.

"You're turning 30!" Mary let out a squeal.

Ruth smiled and rolled her eyes. Maybe she could rearrange that top apple to a different spot. Mary shook her head and hands simultaneously.

"I know what you're thinking," she defended her excitement. "Turning 30 isn't that big of a deal, but Ruth! You're the first person to turn 30 without a husband since our great-grandmum! It's like history all over again! Maybe your husband will come this year, just like Great-Grandmum..." Mary's eyes grew wide with revelation. "Ruth." She jumped and squealed some more remembering that Ruth was named after her great-grandmother. She tried to get her big sister to share in her excitement, and slowly it was beginning to work.

"That's probably not going to happen, Mary." Despite her best efforts to appear uninterested, Ruth had a smile on her face and a laugh in her voice. Mary was 16 and had every right to be excited. She had just been asked to court by young Jonathan Bontrager, and he was the son of the wealthiest man in the community. The Miller family was more than excited to finally have one of their own marry one of the Bontrager boys, especially after everything that had happened with Ruth. It was a little hard for her to be excited because any sign of love gave her more pain. She still had a hard spot on her heart over the way she had been treated by Jacob Bontrager, the eldest of the Bontrager's.

Before Ruth's thoughts could go any further, Mary grabbed her and spun her around. Ruth couldn't contain it anymore; she let out a giggle as they spun around. They almost didn't hear the bells above the door jingle signaling a customer had walked into the store.

"I'll let you get back to work," Mary stated as she headed out the way she came in, seemingly more excited than when she left. Ruth was still by the apple stand and couldn't quite see the door and as soon as she turned the corner, her heart stopped.

Jacob Bontrager was standing before her.

"Hi, Ruth."

That autumn day that he left ten years ago, all she wanted to do was run away. It was hard for her to be focused on helping her younger siblings when she felt like her heart had been ripped out of her chest and stomped on. Jacob Bontrager, the love of her life, had left suddenly with Ruth's very best friend Sarah Yoder. She had found a note outside of her parents' market early that morning addressed to her.

My dearest Ruth, the note began. The time with you has been unmatched. You've made me so happy these past few months and I will always cherish the time we've had together. I have decided to become an Englisher with Sarah Yoder. I know you two were close... please don't hold it against her.

> I hope you can find it in your heart to forgive me,
> Jacob Bontrager

There had been nothing from the couple for the last decade. The families had worried and the community had prayed until one day, Ruth finally told everyone that they needed to let them go. She wasn't a leader in the community by any means, but her strength in the situation had given a lot of people hope and they looked to her for advice on a lot of problems. That's why she enjoyed working alone at her parents' market.

When she saw Jacob standing there, she immediately regretted the fact that she worked alone. She thought of calling her sister Mary back before she had completely left the store, but as soon as the thought crept in, it was slammed out by the jarring noise of the door. It was too late. She was on her own.

"Jacob," was all she could manage. He smiled and her heart fluttered. All she wanted to do was run up and hug him and tell him how much she wished he had at least written once to let her know he was still alive. But the hurt he had caused all those years ago was so great, it kept her glued to her spot on the floor.

"What are you doing here?"

"Isn't it obvious? I want to live here."

"There's nothing here for you. Get out of my store." Her tone shocked even herself, as if someone else had suddenly possessed her body. Jacob looked hurt, but slowly he turned and left the store without another word.

Ruth's breathing was shallow and she had to steady herself on the counter. School was supposed to start next month; she didn't have time to deal with these emotions! First things first, she decided. She needed to talk to her parents about quitting the store.

Ruth's parents were gracious about her decision to leave the store and become a teacher. She assured them this wasn't a new decision, even if it was a little sudden to them.

"We trust your judgment, sweetie," her mother confided to her while they were cleaning up from supper. Usually Mary and Ruth did the dishes together, but Mary asked to be excused from dinner early and hadn't been seen or heard from since. "We're just surprised you waited so long to tell us that this was your plan all along. The old school teacher retired at the end of the school year, and that was almost 2 months ago! What pushed you over the edge?" Ruth put down the glass she was drying and looked her mother square in the face.

"Mama, today I saw Jacob in the store." Her mother almost dropped the bowl she was holding, but Ruth caught it before it hit the floor.

"Oh my word!"

Mama's exclamation brought Ruth's father running into the room. "Is everything alright?" He looked startled. Mama looked at him.

"Ruthy saw Jacob Bontrager at the store today!" Papa looked a little crestfallen at the news that nothing bad was happening, but when what Mama said sunk in, his face went ashen.

"Was Sarah with him?" He asked. She shook her head.

"I told him to leave because I didn't want anything to do with him."

"That's my girl." Papa came over to give her one of his bear hugs.

"But Papa, he said he wanted to live here." She pulled away from the hug to look her parents in the eyes. "Will the community actually forgive him?"

Mama looked at Papa as he slowly nodded. "That's our way, Ruthy. We forgive people who have wronged us, because that's what the Lord asked us to do in His Good Book. Remember, just because you forgive doesn't mean you forget or act as if nothing happened. He still has things to answer for, and not just for the community, but for what he did to you."

Ruth was thoughtful for a moment, but simply nodded and went back to finishing the dishes. She could tell her parents were watching her, but she didn't turn around. Finally she heard her father shuffle away and her mother took her place next to Ruth as they finished the dishes in silence.

The next few weeks of preparations for school were grueling. Normally Mary would be helping Ruth out, but she had been gone a lot these past few weeks. Ruth could only remember seeing Mary a few times over these last weeks. Whenever she asked her parents they never really gave a straight answer.

I just want my sister back, she thought as she opened the door to the schoolhouse.

"SURPRISE!"

Ruth dropped all of the supplies in her arms as the crowd of people standing in the schoolhouse cheered and laughed at her shocked expression. Mary came from somewhere in the crowd and helped her pick up all of her supplies.

"What is this, Mary?" Ruth hissed. "I just want to be a school teacher, not have some party thrown for me!"

Mary smiled. "It's your 30th birthday, silly! I told you it was going to be something special."

Ruth began looking at the amount of people in the house. "How many people are here?"

"As many as I could fit."

Ruth wasn't about to figure out how many that meant. As she stood up, she put on her best smile and took the party in stride.

"Thank you all for coming," she said as everyone quieted down to hear her. "This party was certainly a surprise for me and all of you here has only made it more special. As my sister Mary once said, turning 30 isn't that big of a deal... but it means more when I can share it with people I love." She smiled wide at all of the friends and family in front of her.

"There's cake!" It was Mr. Troyer. Everyone laughed at the old man's exclamation. Ruth went over to give him a hug.

Why not? She thought before declaring, "Let's eat cake!"

There weren't a lot of big parties like this in the community and usually they happened in the church, but Mary knew Ruth would've caught on if she tried to get her to the church in the middle of the week.

"It just happened to work out perfectly that you were coming up here when you did," Mary finished her story.

"Were you just going to have all of these people wait for me for hours?" Ruth couldn't imagine all of these people waiting around hopelessly for her. Mary laughed.

"No, silly! I would've gone and gotten you. But these people would wait for you. In fact, most of them would do almost anything for you."

"What? Why? I didn't do anything special."

Mary shook her head. "Ruthy, Ruthy... because you're a beacon of hope to these people. After Jacob left this community saw you become a real woman who not only doesn't need a man but will help anyone in a tough situation. You pulled this community out of the deepest pits of despair and told us all to follow you to the light.

"You might not see it that way, but they do. And that's what matters most. That's why they showed up today. Not because you're 30, but because you've shown them how to have fun... and they want to remind you to continue to have fun. Especially now that you're old." Mary nudged Ruth as she shook her head at her little sister.

"You're incredible, Mary." Ruth smiled. "Thank you for this." She was quiet for a moment before adding, "Does this mean you'll stop being dodgy now and you can help me get my school ready?" Mary laughed.

"Yes, I will help you get your school ready."

"Good. Now, I'm going to go outside for some fresh air. Jonathan's over there by the cake." Ruth winked at her.

Mary spun around and began making her way in his direction. She stopped mid-step, turned around quickly and gave her sister a hug. "I love you, sissy."

Ruth returned the hug. "I love you, too."

With that, Mary was off to flirt with her beau and Ruth was on her way outside. She had always loved the outdoors. There was no limit to how high or far you could go. After Jacob left, she used to sit outside and wish that the wind would carry her away. As she thought that, the wind suddenly picked up.

"Hi, Ruth."

She spun around. There he was again. Her breathing became shallow again, but she steadied it as she remembered what her father had said about forgiving him.

"Hello, Jacob."

"Oh good. We're on speaking terms." Jacob smiled. It took everything in Ruth to contain herself.

I thought I was over this! "What are you doing here?"

"Wishing you a happy birthday." He attempted to move closer, but she took an equal step back. Thankfully, he took the hint and stopped. He put his hands up in surrender. "Okay. You don't need to be mad."

"How can I not be mad, Jacob?" Ruth suddenly exploded. "You left me for my best friend. On top of that, you left the community altogether! Suddenly after ten years of silence you just want to show up and act as if nothing happened? No, I don't play like that. I will forgive you because it's the right thing to do, but I will *not* forget."

"Why won't you just let me explain myself?" Jacob seemed to be sincerely apologetic.

"What is there to explain? You didn't love me enough. I'll never be good enough for you. Why would I subject myself to that hurt again?" Ruth's voice cracked and she realized she was crying. Jacob's eyes were filled with tears as well and it broke Ruth's heart. But not enough for her to change her position about him.

"I'm so sorry," he began, his voice thick. "You're the only woman that's really shown me what love really is. I just want to talk. One time. I promise you, if you still don't want anything to do with me after that, you will never see me again."

"When? Where?" If this was what it took to get rid of him, she would do it.

"Next Saturday, the church is having a work day. Afterward, they're having a community lunch. We can talk then."

Ruth nodded in response. She was afraid to open her mouth in case her voice betrayed her.

Jacob dipped his head. "Thank you." He turned on his heel and walked off.

The days dragged on as Ruth began to almost dread her meeting with Jacob. Maybe it was a mistake, maybe she should've planned it to be sooner. But no, having other people around was better. No doubt, the community knew he was back. Ruth was surprised she hadn't heard from more people about it.

Mr. Troyer was the first one to bring Jacob up. "So I hear the eldest Mr. Bontrager is back," he began cautiously on Ruth's last day in the store. He searched her eyes before continuing. "People are saying he and the young Ms. Yoder divorced. What have you heard?" Ruth was honestly surprised by that news.

"I haven't heard anything. Jacob wants to talk to me tomorrow after the workday at the church."

"Mmmm," came the response. Ruth hated when Mr. Troyer did that. He always seemed to know more than he was letting on. "Well, dear, I'll tell you this much. You be careful. You can't be a very effective school teacher if you're married."

"But I also can't have children of my own," she shot back. She started to apologize for her bluntness, but the old man simply laughed.

"I've been waiting a long time for you to tell me how you feel. So you want to be married, eh? Well then that's what you'll get." He smiled broadly and shuffled out of the store.

Ruth always seemed confused after certain conversations with Mr. Troyer, but this one topped them all. How did he know she wanted to be married? How did he know she would get married? None of it made sense.

She hoped she would get the answers she was looking for tomorrow.

Ruth came to the workday with her mother and sister to help prepare the food for lunch. Until the night before, she wasn't even aware that they had signed up to help with food. It worked out well though, since she wouldn't have to make an excuse to go. She hadn't told anyone in her family about her planned meeting with Jacob, but Mary had been busy with Jonathan who was clearly shaken about his oldest brother coming home, and Mama had been busy tending for Papa, who had fallen ill suddenly. Mama wanted to blame the food at Ruth's party, but everyone else had eaten the food and no one else was sick. Mama was to call a doctor after the workday; until then, Isaac and his wife Gloria were tending to Papa.

"Come on, Mama," Mary consoled in her usual cheery matter. "Don't worry about Papa! If something happens, they will be sure to let us know!"

"You can worry for me then," Ruth finally admitted. Both women looked at her expectantly. "I'm going to be talking to Jacob after the workday. He's there today and asked if I would be willing to at least listen to what he has to say."

Mary's face registered understanding. "He was who you talked to the day of your birthday when you went outside!"

"Wait, what?" Mama stopped in her tracks. Her daughters stopped as well. "You're telling me you—" she pointed at Ruth—"are going to be talking to Jacob Bontrager. The same man that left you high and dry ten years ago for your best friend?" Ruth nodded. "Why? Why would you do that to yourself, Ruthy?"

"Because..." she hesitated. She'd never said this out loud, not even when he was still a part of her life. "I love him, Mama. And love make you do stupid things, you've said so yourself."

Both Mama and Mary were still shocked about Ruth's confession of love for him, but Mary recovered quickly with a crazy idea.

"Mama! What if..." she waited for special effect. "We both got married to the Bontrager boys! It would be all in the family!" Mary gasped, remembering. "Ruthy! You're 30! It's like Great-Grandmum all over!!!"

Sometimes Mary's excitement was too much, but if it wasn't for her little sister, Ruth's life would be a lot less colorful. Mama looked like she was about to be sick.

"Come on, you two," Ruth coaxed. "We're going to be late if we don't hurry."

The entire workday had this uncomfortable feeling to it. Everyone knew that Jacob was back, and they treated Ruth differently because of it. They were afraid to really talk to her as if she would break down and cry. Ruth hadn't even seen Jacob yet, so she hoped that he was simply staying out of sight.

Jonathan Bontrager came over and made small talk with Mary. Ruth watched their sweet exchange with a hint of longing in her heart. She really did love Jacob, and she had never really stopped. She had caused her heart to become hard because she didn't want to admit the simple fact that she was and always had been head over heels in love with him.

What she really wanted to know was, what happened to Sarah? She and Sarah had been super close growing up; to think that she would simply walk away from everything without a word really didn't sound like her.

Before Ruth knew it, lunchtime was upon them, but Mama wouldn't let Ruth work.

"Go talk to Jacob. He's at the corner table waiting for you."

"How did you—"

"Go!" Mama pushed her in the direction of Jacob.

He was hot and his skin glistened from the exertion of the morning. Instead of beginning the conversation with his usual greeting, he jumped right into his story.

"The bishop is going to give me pardon."

Ruth sat down across from him and waited for more.

"He said you were very strong after we left. You really led the town through the stages of grief and forgiveness like a pro." He looked into her eyes. His deep blue eyes seemed to penetrate into her soul. His dark, black hair was tucked under his hat, as it had been since he'd been back, but she remembered that hair was what caused her to look twice at him the first time they met.

"It wasn't me, it was Christ in me, the hope of glory," she replied by rote. Jacob laughed incredulously.

"You don't even believe that. Look at you, quoting what everyone expects you to hear." He leaned back and stretched before pulling himself closer and leaning toward her. "We both know you thought I was gone for good so you simply told the community to stop grieving. Because *that* sounds more like the Ruth Miller I know. People always claim that Mr. Troyer is the most blunt person here, but we know you're just as bad. You just have more of a filter than he does. But I hear that goes away as you get older. What you need, Ruth, is some freedom."

Ruth shook her head in an attempt to dislodge the strange thoughts that had attached themselves. "I thought you were going to tell me your story, not talk about me."

"But my story starts and ends with you."

Ruth stopped. She looked him in the eye.

"Now that I have your attention, we can begin the story."

Jacob's story

I fell in love with Ruth Miller the first day of kindergarten. There was never a moment that I didn't love her. I knew in my heart of hearts that she would be my wife one day. As the oldest of five boys, I knew that my inheritance was the family business, but I wanted more adventure than staying in the small community and living off of the land. Sarah Yoder, Ruth's best friend, was more of a kindred spirit in that she wanted to explore the world. I managed to become friends with Ruth through Sarah, but it wasn't until Rumspringa *that we really began to pursue a relationship. I realized that being with her was everything that I ever wanted. She was smart, funny, she loved children, and she was devoted to the Lord. Those were qualities I desired for the woman of my dreams. However, Sarah told me one night that the opportunity of a lifetime was about to roll through town and it was for one night only. Sarah had family outside of the Plain community and they were on their way to Philadelphia. They had promised to stop and pick up Sarah so she could go with them. The catch was, Sarah wanted me to go with her. It was almost like a bad dream; I had the choice between the girl of my dreams or the girl of my desires.*

In the moment, I picked the girl of my desires. The city was everything I thought it would be and more. The lights, the sounds, the smells, everything was amazing. And I was getting to do life with at least one of my friends. Within a year, we decided we should get married since we'd been living together already. The first five years of the marriage were pure bliss. I had taken enough money from my father that we didn't have to worry about jobs. We still had side jobs so as not to go completely broke when the money ran out.

As soon as we hit year six of our marriage, I noticed Sarah started to act strange. Suddenly our money was depleting faster than I could manage and I didn't know what was going on. I finally confronted her about it, but she told me to trust her. So I did.

To my shock and horror, I found out where Sarah had been spending the money. She had found another lover and he had been taking her money for his personal gain. When I found out, Sarah suddenly told me she wanted a divorce. She told me she never loved me and only wanted me for my money. Now that my money was gone, I was useless to her. The other man had become very rich off of the money Sarah had stolen from me, and there was no way for me to prove that it was my money he'd used... so I divorced Sarah.

I stayed in Philadelphia a few more years since I still had debt from our very expensive wedding. Everyone told me to use a credit card and build up my credit since I was in my 20s and didn't have any. That was a mistake I will never make. It's a dog-eat-dog world, and I was the one getting eaten alive.

I managed to pay off the rest of the debt and determined there was nothing for me in Philadelphia... so I came back to the community that I call home.

Jacob concluded his story: "It hasn't been easy coming back. So much has changed, but so much is the same. The level of love, compassion and mercy I've experienced has been incredible." He stopped and looked down. "You were the first one that treated me mercilessly... and I knew I was finally getting what I deserved." When he looked up at Ruth, there were tears running down his cheeks. "I didn't think there was any way I could ever forgive myself if you didn't forgive me. I realize that since that first meeting a month ago, you've changed quite a bit already."

"No," Ruth admitted. "I didn't change from that first meeting. I've been changing since the day you left. You were right about me leading this community through the grief. You leaving was the worst thing to happen to us. But the people looked to me because they knew I was hurt the worst. I became bitter for a little while, but Papa told me something that he's had to remind me of over and over throughout these years. He told me that our community is all about forgiveness. We have to let the people we love go in order for them to truly find themselves and discover what they really want. We just hope that what they want is you." Ruth felt tears stream down her cheeks as she continued.

"You think I changed like this overnight, but it took ten years of heartache, grief, and finding myself and my true relationship with God to get me to this point."

Jacob wiped his face with his handkerchief. "Well... I'm glad that you've found your true love again." He stood to leave.

"I have. He's about to leave again." Jacob stopped. He looked back at Ruth. A fresh tear had fallen down his cheek. His eyes looked like the ocean with the tears brimming over his blue eyes.

"You are my true love, Jacob. You always have been. There was never another man in my life because no one could compare to the love and strength that you showed me in the short time we were courting."

"I don't know if I can be that man for you, Ruth. You've grown into this wonderful woman of God who's about to be the teacher of the whole community. I would only be holding you back." Ruth stood and moved around the table until she was inches from Jacob. There were still other people around, but she didn't care. The only thing that mattered was this moment.

"Jacob Bontrager, you will *never* hold me back. It's because of you that I've truly learned how to let go. It's because of you that I decided to become a teacher." She lowered her voice as she moved just a little bit closer to him. His breathing became shallow. "Do you remember what you told me that first day we met in school? When Sarah introduced us?"

Jacob gave a slight nod. "'You have the heart of a teacher. You should use that.'" Ruth smiled.

"You were 5, and you could see that. I'd call that pushing me toward my goal."

Without thinking Ruth closed the small gap to Jacob's mouth with hers. This wasn't an ordinary kiss; there was ten years of heartache and forgiveness in that kiss. All of the words that were unsaid stayed that way. Jacob took Ruth's face in his hands and slowly pulled her away. He was about to say something, but Ruth stopped him.

"I forgive you." His eyes welled with fresh tears that mingled with hers as they kissed again.

Ruth knew in that moment that this was exactly where she needed to be. In his arms. She felt like she was finally home.

6 months later

It was the middle of the school year, but Ruth felt like everyday was the first day. Jacob had worked it out with the bishop to help Ruth teach. It was unprecedented, but there wasn't another teacher lined up who loved the children as much as Ruth did. So they let Jacob stay on as well.

She and Jacob had decided to court again, but they were going to wait until the New Year to marry. Ruth wanted to start a new year with a new husband in a mostly new job. Nobody could blame her;

everything that had gone wrong in her life had turned around for the better.

The only thing that would make it all better is if Ruth would hear from her childhood friend. She was on her way out the front door when Mary stopped her.

"Ruthy! Wait! I forgot to tell you this came for you yesterday while you were out with Jacob." She batted her eyes despite her excitement. Ruth took the envelope Mary held out and looked at it.

"There's no return address."

"I know! Isn't it mysterious?"

"I have to go. I'm going to be late. I'll let you know if it's important." She left her little sister standing by the door, mouth agape.

As Ruth walked, she opened the letter. The postmark said it was from Austin, Texas, but she didn't even really know where that was. As soon as she opened the letter and saw the handwriting, she knew exactly who it was. She had to stop walking, set her stuff down and cry before she could read it.

It was from Sarah!

Dear Ruth,

I'm sure by now you already know this is your very best friend Sarah. I'm sorry for the way I've treated you over these past years. You deserve a better friend than me. Thank you for believing in me even when I didn't deserve to be believed in. One day I will tell you the entire story of what happened, but for now, take this as a promise that I will stay in communication. I love you like a sister. Don't forget about me in your new life (Jacob told me about your engagement; we do still talk on occasion). Congratulations.

Your very best friend,
Sarah Miller

Ruth wiped the tears from her cheeks and ran to the school house. As soon as she got there, she showed Jacob. He simply smiled.

"Yes, we do keep in touch. But only because she still owes me money. Nothing more."

Ruth nodded. She was excited to hear from her very best friend, but overwhelmingly sad that it couldn't have ended differently.

"One day, she'll return," Jacob answered her thoughts. "I know she will. Until then, we have children to teach and a life to get to."

Ruth wiped her face again. Jacob was right. Even though it didn't end the way it should have, she knew that no story was ever fully over. She looked forward to more letters from Sarah... even if she couldn't write back. It was good to finally hear from her friend and to know that her friend would one day make her way back home.

Just like Jacob. This really was what home felt like. And it was good.

An Unlikely Amish Union

Nikki Hamilton had no idea what was about to happen when she decides it was time to discover her past. After her mother's passing, she discovers that she was born Amish. She now wants to know why her mother left the life she was born into. Her adventure to River Stone turns out to be quite an eye opener and she soon discovers that there is a peace there that she would never be able to have in the city. When she meets John Smith, a local farmer from Trumbull, everything changes, and for the first time since her arrival, she's contemplating her future.

John had lost his wife three years ago, and he never once thought that he would ever fall in love again. But against all odds he meets the intriguing Nikki Hamilton, an Englischer with a passion for writing novels. She is eccentric and different, but even with these obstacles and the fact that she's not Amish, he can't keep himself from falling in love. But they are from two different worlds. Is she willing to become Amish?

Translations:

Baremlich = Terrible
Gleh vennigh or gleh bissley — little bit.
Jah – yes

Chapter 1

The tiny creature zoomed about the room like a firefly on steroid. And as small as it was, it wreaked havoc in Clara's tiny little room high up in the attic of the old Steinberg mansion. Down below she could hear the hurried footsteps of Mrs Meremoth, the housekeeper. She grabbed one of her books and swatted at the firefly but it evaded her every move. As it zoomed over her small desk it sent papers flying in all directions. And as Clara was about to burst out in tears everything slowed down. The papers hung in a suspended state in the air and even Mrs Meremoth's footsteps had grown quiet.

Clara fell back on her bed that stood against the wall next to the window and the tiny creature with humanlike features and wings like that of a fly perched on her windowsill.

Awestruck she crawled closer. "Who are you?" she whispered.

"I am Hefeydd, King of the Fae," he announced with his hands planted on his sides.

Clara gasped and her eyes grew wide with wonder. "I don't understand you can't possibly be real." said Clara to the infinitesimal figure perched on her windowsill.

The winged creature laughed, and his laughter shook the window panes despite his miniature size.

"So trifling human girl! Your feeble minds can hardly correlate all the facts and fallacies of your own existence, and you dare doubt ours?"

Clara's brows drew together like the London Tower bridge over the Thames river....

Nikki's fingers flew over the keys of her laptop, she had finally gotten over the writer's block that had been the bane of her existence over the past few weeks, and suddenly her screen died.

"No, no, no, no!" she cried out and banged her hands on the desk. "This cannot be happening!"

She scurried around to find her power supply which she so carelessly discarded earlier when she returned from the library. If she stops now, she's going to lose her inspiration.

She jumped up and hopped on one foot while putting on one shoe then on the other while she tossed the clothes that lay on her bed in all direction searching for her power supply. If she hurried she could get to the market before nightfall to charge her laptop and her power bank. Being it the only place with actual electricity, she had to hurry. Here at her aunt Eva's home in the middle of River Stone, a small Amish village, she was at the mercy of the elements. Other than running water and coal stove, there wasn't really anything, but that was a sacrifice she had been willing to make after discovering her roots.

Shortly after her mother's passing she had discovered that her mother grew up here in River Stone and that she had run away just after her eighteenth birthday and started a life for herself in New Jersey. With her discovery, Nikki couldn't quench her curiosity about this her mother's mysterious past. Since she could remember, her mother never once mentioned her family, which she found odd. Her mother's past had always been a mystery, and it was one she had vowed to unravel against her father's wishes.

With backpack and all, she rushed down the stairs and past her aunt.

"Nicola, where are you going?"

"It's Nikki Aunt Eva, Nikki with a double K and I'm just going to the market real quick."

For the life of her she couldn't understand why her aunt insisted on calling her Nicola when her name was Nikki.

"But it's almost lunch time dear," her aunt protested.

"I'll be back soon, I promise," Nikki persisted and rushed out the door.

There was no way anyone was going to prevent her from getting her laptop charged. She was already committed to spend the evening writing so that she could get this Novel done and stopping now will set her back at least a day. A deadline was a deadline.

John was about half a mile away from the market, his carriage loaded with fruits and vegetables from his farm back in Trumbull when suddenly his carriage jerked and his horses stalled. It was already past lunch time, and he had hoped to be at the market almost two hours ago. But delays on the road, had kept him, and now on top of it, the carriage wheel had separated from the carriage. Frustrated, he got off and walked around to the right side of the carriage to inspect the damage. He really didn't expect this to happen, but then again, he hardly did any maintenance on his carriages. When he didn't farm, he spent his days behind books reading, anything from historical books to modern Englisch biographies. This will teach him, he thought disappointedly. He was going to have to walk the rest of the way to River Stone and find one of the locals to come and help him.

He had just collected his belongings when the sound of a scooter drew closer, in the distance he could see the rider was a female, but the way her hair waved in the wind from under the helmet. It was obvious by her clothes that she was also an Englischer. Not expecting much help, he turned and started to walk but instead of the rider whizzing past she stopped.

"Do you need any help?" she asked from behind the visor.

"Um, I don't think so, my wheel split I just need to get to River Stone market."

The woman removed her helmet and John held his breath. She was beautiful, he was not going to deny that, but he knew better than to want.

"I can give you a ride; I'm heading to the market, anyway."

John contemplated this; he was losing time as it was, and if he could get to the market sooner than later, he could at least find someone to help him before night fall. He glanced at the scooter and then back at his wagon filled with fruit and vegetables.

"If it's no trouble," he said tentatively.

She waved her hand and smiled, "No problem at all, hop on."

John awkwardly moved to get on the back of the scooter, with little space he was sitting up against her back with his hands on her shoulders.

"Hold on," she warned and put her helmet back on before starting her scooter.

As she pulled away, he jerked and nearly flew off the back but managed to regain his grip. Within twenty minutes or so, they reached River Stone and the young woman pulled to a stop near the warehouse.

"Well, here we are," she said and waited for him to get off, before she got off.

"Thank you."

"No problem."

And without waiting she dashed into the warehouse.

What an odd character, he thought as he watched her disappear. She was completely out of place here at River Stone, yet she seemed like she was comfortable among the Amish. He couldn't help but wonder if she was some sort of reporter who like so many, visited Amish villages to get a scoop on their lives.

"I see you've met Eva's niece."

"Abraham!" John greeted and shook his friend's hand, "She's not Amish though."

"No, she isn't, not yet anyway, but she's made herself at home."

Abraham chuckled and crossed his arms. "So pray tell, how on earth did you manage to get on the back of that thing?"

John rubbed the back of his head and sighed. "My carriage broke down about a two miles outside of town. And this young lady came to my rescue."

"I see, well, let's go and get your produce, and I'll arrange for one of my boys to go see to the carriage and the horses."

"Thanks."

The two men were off in no time, but John couldn't get the red head out of his mind. She intrigued him, and he wanted to find out more about her.

Chapter 2

The warehouse was more like a local grocer; the walls were lined with shelves containing various preserved items like preserved lemons, apricots, beans, and mixed veggies. And of course her favourite, sweet and sour preserved figs. Towards the back of the warehouse were homemade dresses and tea towels, quilted blankets and cute little doilies with beaded edges. Something she had never seen in her life, but Aunt Eva used them over all her containers in her kitchen.

She darted for the counter and plastered her most amiable smile on her face.

"Good afternoon Mrs Troyer, isn't it a lovely day today?"

Mrs Troyer raised a brow, but a smile tugged at the corners of her mouth. "Indeed, it's a lovely day to spend outside and get to meet a few people."

Nikki cringed inwardly. Mrs Troyer had been trying to get her more involved at the market, but right now she had a deadline.

"I promise by Friday I'll be out and about, I just need to finish the last few chapters of my book, would I be able to use your power again?"

"Nikki, you should put that thing away and take time to get to know the surrounding people. You bury your face in that monstrosity and it isn't good."

Nikki sighed and bit her lip, "I know, I just need to get my work done before I can actually spend time enjoying this wonderful place."

Mrs Troyer wiped her hand on her apron and gestured with her head. "I'll be closing shop early, so don't waste any time."

"Oh thank you! I really owe you big time."

Nikki headed to the back where she could plug her laptop in. She felt bad for using Mrs Troyer's electricity but every time she offered to pay, Mrs Troyer wanted to hear nothing of it. But she was adamant to contribute one way or the other. As soon as her book was finished, she promised herself she would come and give Mrs Troyer a hand and help her to stock up her shelves or something.

She settled behind her laptop and continued to write her book. It amazed her how her writers block had flown out the window the day she arrived here at River Stone. Back home, there were far too many distractions. Her apartment block was one of the rowdiest places, with couples squabbling on either side of her. Above her, her neighbours sounded like they were doing Irish dancing on wooden floors. Just after her mother's passing, she had learned that her mum used to be Amish. It was all in a letter her mum had left behind for her. From that she had learned that her mother left River Stone shortly after her sixteenth birthday when she couldn't take living here anymore. She had been on her Rumspringa and had met a young man, whom she had fallen in love with at the time. Completely smitten she was willing to sacrifice her life in the Amish community to explore the possibilities of modern life. It never worked out with this young man, but her mother refused to go back to her former life, and ended up staying in Ohio, where she eventually met her dad. This too didn't work out as planned. Shortly after her birth, her biological father ran off with some floozy and her mother was left to raise her all on her own. With no real education other than the minimal schooling she had here in River Stone, her mother worked two jobs at the local Walmart and coffee shop, just so that Nikki could go to school and finally study further. Her mother really gave her all and for that she was grateful. But Nikki couldn't help but wonder what it would have been like if her mum returned when she was still a baby.

Knowing that she could have grown up Amish, had her wonder what her life would have been like. It took her almost a year to track Aunt Eva down, and when she did, she impulsively jumped at the opportunity to find out for herself, why her mother decided that modern life was far better than the Amish. The information she had gathered the weeks before she finally packed her bag, was all hearsay. Articles on websites and blogs that sounded a little farfetched, not to mention the whole conspiracy that the Amish believe that the earth is flat, and that the devil hides in every electronic device.

Three hours later, she had finished the last few chapters of her book. Her creativity was blossoming, and all it needed now was editing. She attached her document in her email to her editor and sent it off.

Now, she could finally just relax and as Mrs Troyer insisted, experience the Amish life.

She glanced around her and her eyes fell on a lilac dress hanging on one of the rails. Maybe she should embrace the life in full for a while, walk in her mother's footsteps and see for herself what the Amish were about.

Chapter 3

The various stalls lined the market place and John was pleased that he had managed to get all his fresh produce here in time. It was the second day since he arrived, and despite the rain that had been pouring down none stop, he had made good revenue on his sales. By the end of the week he would have enough money to purchase more wood to build his shed back home. His heart cramped in his chest. To this day, three years after his wife's passing he still felt the tug in his heart when he thought of her. Mary always wanted a shed where she could work on her paintings, and he had promised to build her one for years, but never had the means. It was his promise to her at the time of her death that he would finish the shed as he promised.

"It's a *baremlich* day!" Abraham exclaimed as he ducked in under the cover where John has his stand.

"*Gleh vennigh or gleh bissley,* but we should be thankful for the rain."

"*Jah* I guess we need the rain. So have you sold much?"

"*Jah*, plenty, it's been a good season."

Abraham grinned and picked up one of the red starling apples, "Das gut, "he said and took a bite. "So will you be staying here much longer?"

John nodded, "Until the end of the week, but I will be back at the end of the month."

"Good to know, so you can join us for the grain harvest."

John grinned, he enjoyed those gatherings most of all. It's when everyone in the area gets together and helps with the thrashing. It's one of the annual events where everyone gets to frolic and enjoy each other's company.

"I'll definitely be here then."

"Excuse me," a woman's voice sounded behind him and when he turned around he was caught slightly off guard.

The young woman who helped him just yesterday stood before him wearing a Lilac dress with a white apron and a cap. She was quaintly transformed from Englisch to Amish and his heart impulsively skipped a beat. Abraham cleared his throat and made some random excuse to escape leaving him alone with the woman.

"How may I help you?" he asked attempting to sound casual.

"I see you managed to get your stuff here," she said smiling.

"Jah, I did. Thank you for bringing me to town."

"Oh it wasn't a bother at all."

Her smile lit up her grey eyes, and he had to force himself to look away, the last time he had noticed a woman was when he first met Mary, and having these feelings towards a complete stranger felt oddly out of place.

"Are you here to buy fruits or vegetables?" he asked curiously.

She smiled and looked at the crates. "Yes, I'm actually looking for some carrots and potatoes. Aunt Eva said I must come and see you."

"Well then I can most certainly help you there."

John reached for a woven basket and handed it to her. "Feel free to help yourself; the carrots are nice and sweet."

"I wouldn't know the first thing about vegetables," she said, and he noticed the slight blush on her cheeks.

"Right, well, it's all ripe and ready."

John bent down and picked up a bunch of carrots, "Did Eva say how many she wanted?"

"Oh... no she just said I must get some."

"Well why don't you take two bunches, they will last at least two weeks if she doesn't use it all today. And then a bag of potatoes will last her a while too."

"My name is Nikki Hamilton, by the way," she introduced.

Embarrassed he dusted his hands off and extended one hand to her, "I'm sorry, it was rude of me. My name is John."

"Just John?" she asked taking his hand.

"John Smith."

"Well John Smith, it's a pleasure to meet your acquaintance. How much do I owe you?"

John rambled off the amount and Nikki paid him. She was about to turn and leave when he jumped at the opportunity.

"Here let me help you."

"Oh no, it's fine, I'm parked all the way at the warehouse."

She sounded surprised, and he smiled. "It's fine, the stuff is heavy, I'll carry it for you."

"But you can't leave your stall unattended."

He frowned amusedly, realizing that she was worried about his goods.

"Yes I can," he smiled and flipped the sign board that read '*Be back in 15 min*'.

"What if your produce goes missing?" she asked alarmed and clung to her basket.

"My dear, this is not the city, people here are honest and they don't steal from the hand that feeds them."

By the surprised look on her face, he could tell she was amused. So he gently pried the basket from her hand and waited for her to follow him.

"I must admit, seeing you in Amish clothes is rather odd."

Nikki raised a brow and laughed, "Well I figured if I'm going to experience the Amish ways, I can't hold back."

The way John smiled caused a flutter in her stomach and she could feel a blush flood her cheeks.

"If you really want to experience an Amish adventure, you should get rid of your scooter."

"Oh heavens no, how will I get around?"

"You need a horse drawn buggy."

She laughed then. "Me driving a buggy, I doubt that would end well."

"Why so?"

"I'm afraid of horses," she admitted, "Or they are afraid of me, either way, we don't get along."

"I highly doubt that's the case, you just need to understand them."

They reached her scooter, and John took the liberty to fasten her basket on the carry rack on the back. She was keenly aware of him, and couldn't help but find him rather attractive although he was dressed very simple with his broadfall pants, blue shirt and suspenders. But there was something about him, something she couldn't quite put her finger on. His eyes were a deep brown and there was sadness in his eyes, but his smile was genuine.

Chapter 4

It had been a week since Nikki had met John, and he had gone on his way, back to his home town. But for some reason she couldn't get him out of her mind. He was so unlike the men she knew back home. He was kind, hospitable and a true gentleman. Taking into account that her most recent failed relationship had been with a body builder who had a bad attitude, meeting John was like the flip side of the coin.

"Aunt Eva?" she said one morning when they were having breakfast.

"Yes dear?"

"How well did you know my mother?"

Aunt Eva got up and took her dishes to the sink. "Your mother was a free spirit, she didn't believe in the restrictions of the Amish ways."

"And do you believe in these restrictions?"

Her aunt came to sit with her. "I'm still here," she smiled. "Your mother was young, and foolish. She chased after things of the world and I can't blame her. When we went on our Rumspringa, she met a boy, and she was instantly infatuated by his promises."

Nikki cupped the mug in her hands and looked at the coppery tea with the lemon floating inside of it. If this place had been so peaceful why would her mother have chosen another path? She thought about the things she had experienced thus far; friendly faces, casual frolics with the other Amish girls and learning, for the first time, how to quilt. Life here in this small Amish village was just too peaceful, it simply made no sense.

She sat quietly for a while and Aunt Eva started clearing the dishes.

"Will you be coming to church with me?" she asked.

Nikki nodded, "Sure, is it this evening?"

"Yes, at around six tonight, I think you'll enjoy it."

Her aunt was so excited, if she had to compare Eva to her mother, they were two completely different people.

"I'm sure it will be fun, what are your plans today?" she asked.

"I'm going to Mary to finish a few quilts; you're welcome to come along."

Nikki smiled and shook her head, she had other plans. There was a room in the house that was totally deserted. Aunt Eva made sure to keep the door closed at all times, and it was off limits for her, but perhaps she can find some more information about her mother and why she left in that room.

As soon as Aunt Eva had left, Jane made her way up the stairs to the top floor. Naturally her adrenalin was pumping as she approached the room at the end of the hallway. She slowly turned the door knob, and the door swung open. The curtains were drawn, and the room was covered in dust. On the small desk to the left of the tidy bed stood a vase with dead flowers, and next to it was a post card. Nikki leaned over, careful not to disturb the current state of the room and looked at the postcard. She couldn't make out what it said, it was written in Dutch, but at the bottom of the postcard was her mother's name with a small heart drawn next to it. The only thing she could make out was that it was addressed to Eva.

She looked around and tried to find more clues as to why her mother left, but there was nothing of value. Other than a normal few items of clothing, and books, it seemed like her mother has a very normal life. She was about to leave the room when she noticed the corner of a poster sticking out behind the closet. She carefully moved the closet away from the wall and reached behind it. It was an A4 sized poster of the Annie stage production at Broadway 1992—two years before she was born. On the border of the poster was scribbled—*I will go there.* The handwriting was the same as that on the post card.

It all suddenly made sense. Her mother must have seen this play and decided that the glamour of the city was far more appealing than the Amish life she had led. Once she had come to that conclusion she quietly left her mother's room and closed the door behind her. She had to admit, she half expected something far more sinister to come from this, but all it was, was that her mother had a dream, and she gave up her life to follow her dream. Not that she became a famous actress, but she got to see the world.

Chapter 5

As the days passed, Nikki's impatience for feedback from her editor started to dissipate more and more. Her phone now discarded in the bedside drawer next to her bed, and her laptop forgotten in the back of the wardrobe. She'd become more involved with the community, visiting the local school, joining in on various events hosted by the women in the community, and her weekly visit to church and frolicking sings had become the pinnacle of her everyday life here in River Stone. For the first time in her life, she wasn't chasing after impossible deadlines and annoying editors who insisted on show rather than tell scenes, especially when showing was completely irrelevant in the progress of the plot. But needless to say, her keen interest in a certain member of the Amish community was also the reason she so thoroughly enjoyed everything. John Smith, although not from River Stone, was an esteemed member nonetheless and there was something about him that intrigued Nikki. He was soft spoken with impeccably refined manners, which was in total contrast of his strong manly features. She could spend hours just watching him at his stall, loading heavy crates of fruits and vegetables into buyers' buggies. Every now and again she had to force herself not to stare, especially now that she was helping out at the condiments stand, where Mrs Troyer roped her in to help her sell her jams and honey.

But even so, the occasional shy smile from John now and again, did not go unnoticed. There was definitely something brewing there, and it was only a matter of time before something extraordinary hatched. Then again, Nikki's romantic side often blinded her to the harsh realities of life. It's just that here in this community everything was so real and so transparent.

"If you stare any longer, you'll set that stall on fire." A deep timber voice spoke beside her.

Ripped out of her reverie, she cleared her throat and scrambled for a tea towel.

"I'm sorry, my mind was elsewhere, how may help you?" she said plastering a smile on her face at the man standing in front of her.

"The name's Abraham," he said with a wide grin.

"Pardon?" she asked confused.

"You're Nikki right, Eva's niece?"

Get it together, she reprimanded herself and shifted her weight. "Um... yes, I'm Nikki," she said half embarrassed. "Can I interest you in any of Mrs Troyer's jams?"

He laughed and shook his head, then pointed to the honey-nut-brittle snacks. It was then that she noticed the young boy standing next to him.

"Oh I see," she grinned and looked over the edge of the table at the blonde haired boy, "You have a sweet tooth don't you?

The boy nodded, with his thumb stuck in his mouth and Nikki handed Abraham a jar of candy.

"He fancy's you."

Nikki's hand froze and clutched the jar of candy tighter. "I'm sorry?"

"John. He lost his wife three years ago, I thought he'd never move on, but I can see he fancy's you."

Nikki felt a blush creep to her cheeks, and she fumbled with her apron, averting her gaze every which way. "I'm sure you're imagining things," she muttered under her breath.

"I see the obvious. You like him too *jah*?"

Nikki's eyes grew wide, was it that obvious to the surrounding people? She dared to glance past him, half expecting John to be looking her way, but he was busy with a customer.

"He's a fine gentleman, but I'm not sure about your assumptions."

Abraham didn't utter another word, simply smiled and tipped his hat before walking off with his son. Nikki's heart was beating a million miles a second. She had only spoken to John a few times; it was hardly ground for a relationship of any sorts. And worst of all, now it was even harder to keep her eyes off John. Her curiosity to see if Abraham was indeed right, overrode her sanity. And by the end of the day, she had spent every ounce of control to keep herself from staring at him all day. Needless to say, she hastily packed up the stall and rushed home, just to get away from the heated tension that was so obviously brewing between them, and worst of all, they didn't have to say a single word.

John had to do everything in his power to stay true to Mary, although she had been dead for over three years, he couldn't deny the obvious attraction he felt towards this new girl. And he had noticed just after Abraham's visit to her stall, she had grown overly clumsy, but also noticed that she kept looking his way. Abraham was the one who told him that Nikki fancied him, and at first he didn't want to believe him. What would a beautiful Englischer who wrote fantasy novels for a living want to do with a boring Amish man? He had done his homework on her, and with the help of Eva, he had found out all he needed to know about her. And even though a union between him and the Englischer was out of the question and practically impossible, he could not deny the feelings he had started to develop for her.

This afternoon however, unlike other afternoons, Nikki had rushed to get home and John couldn't help but wonder if it was too presumptuous of him to think that she fancied him. Maybe he misinterpreted her occasional smile in his direction, and all it was, was curiosity.

"John dear," Eva said when she came walking along the path towards his stall where he had already packed all his produce away in crates.

"Eva, it's rather late for you, shouldn't you be home?"

The old woman smiled and held out her hand. "I can be wherever I want to be at whatever time," she said stubbornly.

"That is true, so how can I help you?"

Eva blushed and shrugged. "Well you see, I'll be staying over at Gretchen's place tonight to help with the baby, her daughter has finally gone into labour, so I was wondering if you could go by the house and just let Nikki know."

Surprised, John cocked a brow. He sniffed a plot brewing here, but he nodded anyway. "Of course, when can she expect you back?"

"Who knows, babies come when they want, we can only wait."

He laughed and stacked the last of his crates on top of the others. "I'll let her know," he agreed with a smile.

Eva turned to leave and then stopped, "Oh and maybe you can take her some dinner, I haven't cooked, and these city girls don't have the foggiest on what to do in a kitchen."

If ever there was a clever plot, he thought amused, but even then he felt the small flutter of butterflies deep down in the pit of his stomach.

Chapter 6

Nikki looked up at the cuckoo clock against the wall. Aunt Eva was never this late, and she was starting to get worried and frustrated. She had no idea where to even start looking if she had to go find her aunt. She paced the living room impatiently and kept looking out the window, but there was no sight of her aunt.

Irritated, Nikki went to the kitchen, opening cupboard to find some food to start cooking. Other than vegetables, there wasn't much else. In the pantry she found some beans and eggs. How on earth Aunt Eva managed to always cook such delicious dinners with so little at her disposal, was beyond her, she thought as she flopped down on one of the chairs in the kitchen? Just then someone knocked on the door and she didn't think twice to go and open it, only to be shocked to find John standing there with a dish in his hand.

"Good evening," he said politely and shrugged holding up the dish. "I come bearing gifts."

Nikki gaped at him at first before she realized, she looked like a complete idiot.

"Do come in," she said and stepped aside. "I have no idea where Aunt Eva is, but you can put it in the kitchen."

"Eva is over at Gretchen's house, her daughter is having her baby and she's helping the midwife."

Nikki closed the door behind her but didn't dare move, simply watched John disappear into the kitchen before she finally followed. When she entered the kitchen he had already taken out two plates and two glasses.

"She sent me to bring you some food, and let you know she would be home very late, if at all."

Being alone in a house with John made her feel giddy and watching him move about the kitchen as if he belonged there was even more intriguing. The men she knew back home were complete brute's who cared about nothing but themselves.

"Your aunt told me you write novels," he said casually.

So they've been talking about her, she thought and a kaleidoscope of butterflies fluttered about in her stomach. "Well sort of, but I haven't touched anything since the first day I ran into you."

John stopped mid dishing up food and looked at her. "Why have you stopped?"

Nikki pulled herself together and took the salt and pepper shaker and put it on the table. "For one, electricity is a problem, and a laptop relies on that. Secondly, I'm waiting for a new contract, but I've grown tired of the type of novels I'm expected to write."

He continued dishing up food and then pulled out her chair for her. "And what do you want to write?"

She shrugged as she sat down. "I don't quite know to be honest; I just need some inspiration I guess."

"I see, well I'm sure you'll find inspiration once you're back in the city."

Before she could reply, John bowed his head and said grace. She was too consumed by him to bow her head, and when he said Amen and looked up at her, it was almost as if time went into a suspended state. It was John who severed the current between them when he finally looked away and reached for the salt.

"It's cottage pie. Eva said you like it."

Completely unnerved by the moment they shared earlier, she fumbled with her fork and nodded. "I do, and it's also the only thing I can make."

"You can't cook?"

She blushed and looked down at her plate. "I lived off microwave dinners and very basic meals like, instant noodles, scrambled eggs and toast."

John chuckled and her stomach tumbled wildly. The rest of the evening they spent talking about her life in the city. How she became a writer and what had driven her to come to River Stone. John told her about his wife and how hard it had been for him to finally let her go. But somewhere in between she realized that she wasn't only falling in love with life in River Stone, and its simple but practical ways, she had started to develop feelings for John.

By around eight that evening and after they shared a cup of tea, John finally got up and helped her to clear the dishes.

"Tell me something," she started nervously.

"What do you want to know?"

"Is it a sin for a man and woman who aren't, you know, together, to be alone in a house?"

The amused look on John's face made her smile, and when he laughed, she laughed.

"We're not sixteen anymore. Things are different for widows and adults in the Amish community. Why do you ask?"

Nikki blushed profusely and turned away to hide her face from him, and as casually as she could she said, "I was just wondering in general, that's all."

She felt him standing close behind her and she a shiver of anticipation ran down her spine.

"Is that really all, or are you willing to admit there's something going on between us?"

With that she spun around and gasped, "That's absolutely ludicrous! We're complete opposites."

The moment the words were out, she regretted them, but when John didn't react shocked or hurt by her words, she took a deep steadying breath. "What I mean is that we're two completely different individuals. Whatever is going on between us, is... is, actually I have no idea what it is."

John folded the dish towel and set it down on the sink before turning to her. "To be honest, I don't know either, but I'm not one to ignore the obvious. My father used to tell me, if something feels right, and there is no sin to be committed, then it's the path you are destined to follow."

Nikki was speechless, but instead of going after him, she let him go.

"What on earth just happened?" she said loudly as she pressed the heels of her palms against her eyes.

Chapter 7

A week had passed and John had been busy on his own farm making sure everything was ready. The shed he had promised to build Mary was finally finished, and all that was left to do was furnishing it. It was a small little building made out of wood, with a thatched roof, something he hadn't done before, but it worked out well. The front of the shed had a large open window that overlooked the creek down below, and the scenery was something out of this world. He always loved nature and having this piece of land was perfect for him. When he and Mary had gotten married, they had such high hopes to have a family, but she could not bear any children. Even then, he was happy to grow old with the love of his life and have nieces and nephews visit the farm instead. But since then things have changed, although he thought fondly of Mary, he no longer felt lost and bereft. It was a chapter in his life that had come to an end and the time had come for him to move on to the next chapter.

He arrived in River Stone shortly after ten on the Sunday morning. Everyone was still at the church service, which he had missed due to a detour he had taken, but it was worth his while. He headed straight to Eva's house to wait for them to return from church.

Not long after, the two women came strolling up the path towards the house. From where he stood, he could see the smile on Eva's face and in turn the uncertainty on Nikki's.

"John, what a lovely surprise dear boy, what brings you to River Stone on a Sunday?" Eva said when they drew closer.

John smiled and greeted Eva and then looked at Nikki.

"I'm actually here to see Nikki, can you give us a moment?" he asked, never taking his eyes off of her.

"I'm sure we can all get a cup of tea inside," Nikki protested.

Eva laughed, "Nicole, why don't you go with John and I'll get the tea ready."

John simply smiled at her and he could see the nervousness in her eyes.

Nikki felt her heart do a gazillion leaps as she stood facing John. After their whole debacle in the kitchen a week ago, all she could think about was him. She hashed out every possible reason why they could never be together, but each time her heart ached, knowing she would be losing more than a chance at happiness. She was a writer, not a house wife or a cook. She wasn't like any of the other women in the Amish community, and that was exactly what John needed, a good Amish wife that could cook and sew.

"What do you want?" she blurted out abruptly.

John looked at her and smiled and that was another thing that frustrated her. No matter how rude she was or how direct she tried to be, he seemed oblivious to her intensions.

"I want to show you something," he said quietly, "But you'll have to come for a ride with me."

"A ride where?"

"To my farm, out at Trumbull, it's a few miles north."

Confused she looked back at the house, "But Aunt Eva is making tea."

"That's fine, we can have tea, but I would really like you to come with me, I promise to bring you back home."

She should have said no, but she couldn't, and an hour later, she was sitting next to John in his buggy heading to his farm. The ride to Trumbull was pleasant, but she could hardly breathe at the rate her heart was beating in her chest. All along the way John introduced her to the farms along the road side, giving her some insight on every family who lived there and shared some historical facts about the area.

He finally turned into a narrow road, and up ahead, the farmhouse stood on the hill. It looked like it had always been a part of the pale green hills that surrounded it. A beautiful white wooden house, box shaped with a blue door dead centre. There were square windows on either side of the house with matching blue shutters flung open invitingly. The path that leads to the house was made of stone and snaked up from the small gate to the front door. It was nothing short of magnificent in its own peculiar way. Almost instantly, Nikki had a plot for a novel brewing in her mind. Being here in Trumbull at John's farm had awakened her creativity again, but this time it had nothing to do with dragons and fairies.

"Here we are," he said drawing her back to reality.

"This is your house?" she asked awestruck.

"Yes, but I'll show the house in a bit, I want to show you something else."

A flutter of excitement swirled up inside of her as she followed him around the back of the house to a small shed that stood a few feet away from the main house. Past the shed was a small patch of trees that lead down into a creek. It was a complete sensory overload.

"This way," he said and took her around to the entrance.

"I'm not sure why you brought me here," she finally admitted.

"I wanted to show you were I live, wait here and have a look around."

Without a word he disappeared, leaving her in the small cabin. In front of the large window was a desk. To her right a book shelf, with a few books. Against the one wall were two matching chairs, with floral printed cushions and a small table between them.

It was a cosy little nook where a person could simply hide away from reality, she thought as she took it all in. What was even more beautiful was the view. The hills sloped down from the mountain and dove into the creek not too far from the small cabin and from where she stood she could hear the rushing water down below.

John appeared a few minutes later and placed a box on the desk. "I found this, and I thought you might like it."

A small frown formed between her brows as she looked down at the box and she bit her lip. She had no idea what John had gotten her, but whatever it was, it belonged in this cabin, and that can only mean one thing. The though alone had her mind spinning.

He opened the box and then pulled out a vintage Olivetti typewriter and her heart melted.

"You got me a type writer?" she asked in shock.

He smiled and placed it in the centre of the desk. "I did, the thing is, I want you to write, it's who you are. I don't expect you to be a domesticated housewife. There is no denying that I'm in love with you. Every day I wake up and all I see is you and I figured if you can come here, write to your hearts content, I can make you happy."

Nikki's eyes shot full of tears, and she clasped her hands in front her mouth. She was officially speechless.

"If you don't want me I'll understand," John said and this time she could see he was also nervous.

She walked towards the type writer and ran her fingers over the bubble keys that sloped upwards. If anything she would have given up writing if it meant being with John. But now, this gesture on its own had proven to her that he was willing to accept her regardless so their differences.

She slowly turned to him and smiled, tears glimmering in her eyes. "I didn't think you would approve of the fact that I'm a writer, or of the fact that I have no idea how to cook anything other than Cottage Pie."

John laughed and reached for her hands and brought them to his lips. "I can teach you how to cook, if you teach me how to use a type writer."

Nikki laughed and cried all at once, and John pulled her into his arms. "Yes," she whispered, and John gently kissed her tears from her cheeks.

"I have a generator, so you can bring your laptop too."

With that Nikki flung her arms around his neck and clung to him. So overwhelmed with emotion that she wasn't sure if she would ever recover, she pressed her lips against his.

~*~

"Cloe is such a darling name," Aunt Eva said as she bounced the little dark haired girl on her lap, "But it's not really that Amish."

Nikki laughed and brought the spoon full of baby food to her little girl's mouth. "John named her, if anything it's as Amish as it will ever get."

The trio sat in the meadow outside of the cabin while Nikki fed Cloe, Aunt Eva sat holding the precious little girl on her lap and John worked on building the tree house for his little girl to play on.

"Do you think she'll like it?" he called from the first treehouse.

"She'll love it!" Nikki called and smiled at her husband.

Just over a year ago, she would never have through herself to be a wife, much less a mother, but in a blink of an eye all of that had changed. With John's help she managed to publish her very first book on 'Becoming Amish'. It was their story, of how relentless love can overcome any diversity between two people who are destined to be together.

Ruth 1:16-17

16 But Ruth replied, "Don't urge me to leave you or to turn back from you. Where you go I will go, and where you stay I will stay. Your people will be my people and your God my God. 17 Where you die I will die, and there I will be buried. May the Lord deal with me, be it ever so severely, if even death separates you and me."

AMISH SUNSET

NANCY MANN

72

Chapter I

Rain decorated the grassy fields of Lancaster County. The sky was a cloud grey, the sun remaining absent as the county mourned for the loss of William Bradshire, a carpenter that had been known throughout the county for his kindness and love towards the people around him.

Friends and family had gathered in the county's cemetery for William's funeral, one of the mourners being William's love, Mary Lee Warner. Out of everyone there, Mary was the most damaged from it. William's parents had passed on early in his life due to illnesses and the remaining family he had weren't as close. If anything, Mary was the only one there who truly was family to him.

As Bishop David spoke about his memories with William, Mary thought to herself how God could do such a thing, to take away an innocent being this early in his life. William was only in his mid-twenties, like Mary. He had so much to experience in his life, but it was stripped away from him so early due to the accident.

"If anyone has anything to say, speak now." Bishop David said, stepping back and letting anyone step forward to speak.

There was a long pause, silence being present as Mary thought to herself. Eventually, she took a step forward, standing in front of the casket as she let out a depressed sigh.

"William...had a beautiful soul," Mary said quietly, holding onto a wildflower, "a soul that I have yet to find in any other human being."

Everyone was watching her speak, seeing what Mary had in her hand and what she had to say about William being gone.

"I can't imagine not meeting him in my life...all the memories we've made together...all the laughter, the love...I'm going to miss it." Mary spoke as tears ran down her cheeks. "I don't know if I will find another William in my life."

Some of William's family members began to have tears fall too as they listened to Mary's words about their lost kin. Mary soon stepped back from the casket, having finished speaking on the behalf of William's death. Bishop David soon stepped forward again, wiping some tears from his own eyes.

"Thank you Mary...I will say, before I close in prayer, that it will be difficult to find another William in our lives." Bishop David said to Mary before opening his Bible.

Verses from the Bible were soon spoken out loud, everybody bowing their heads in prayer as Bishop David spoke. While everyone listened, Mary wasn't listening to the verses, in fact, she was in her own mind at this point.

"Why God...why would you take William away from me?" Mary thought to herself. *"William didn't even get half way into his life...why would you take him now?"*

As she struggled with the idea of William passing on, Bishop David finished reading the verses, quietly speaking the word *amen* as he closed his Bible, everybody soon leaving the scene of the funeral, letting the casket to be lowered into the grave. While the casket lowered, Mary was the only one present, witnessing her love's final presence on the surface of Earth.

In regards to funeral traditions of the Amish, flowers were not placed on the casket. For Mary though, traditions meant nothing to her in this occasion. She took the wildflower that she was holding in her hand and tossed it down into the undug grave, letting it land on the coffin before the gravediggers began to bury the coffin.

"I love you so much William." Mary said as the coffin soon disappeared from the soil piling on top. Tears continued to fall onto the soil as she left the site of the funeral.

Chapter II

Several years later...the county had returned back to its normal ways, except for Mary. Ever since William passed away, Mary wasn't her old self. Her old cheerful personality had passed on as well, leaving her a closed up, emotionless woman in her mid-twenties.

She tried to return back to a normal life by going to church, seeing if God might be able to help her find peace, but the more she went the church, the more she began to question God. At times, she would find herself being angry at God for taking William away this early in his life. Eventually, Mary stopped going to church, which brought the concern of Bishop David, leading him to go to Mary's home.

Her house was a little way from town, being near one of the farms. She lived in a large house that belonged to William and his parents. Now that William passed on, Mary now owned the house and lived in it by herself.

Bishop David knocked on the front door, waiting for it to be opened. It took a few knocks before the door finally opened, Mary standing there in a stone grey dress.

"Yes?" Mary quietly said, looking at him with her expressionless face.

"May I come in?" Bishop David asked softly, his expression being hopeful that she would accept his request.

Mary let out a quiet sigh before she nodded, stepping out of the way for Bishop David to come in.

"Thank you...Mary." He said, soon walking into her home, looking around.

Mary shut the door behind Bishop David, walking past him and sitting down on a chair in the living room, continuing what she was doing before he knocked. When Bishop David sat down across from her, he noticed that she was knitting a quilt.

"Oh...I see that you've been busy with making a quilt." Bishop David said, giving Mary a gentle smile.

"Quilts. I've been busy making quilts." She said quickly, pointing in the corner to a basket of several quilts.

Bishop David was surprised by the amount of quilts she had made. "That's quite the number of quilts Mary." He said with a small laugh after.

Mary raised her eyebrows as she continued to knit the quilt. "I've found that work is one of the few things that keeps me from thinking about the past." She said softly, not making eye contact with Bishop David.

"Oh...well...if that's what helps you find peace." He said quietly, rubbing the back of his neck before he finally decided to talk about why he wanted to talk to her. "Mary...I'm worried about you."

She heard Bishop David, stopping for a second before she continued knitting the quilt. "Why?" Mary questioned him.

"I'm concerned for you because you haven't been going to church for months." Bishop David finally said, looking at her with a worried expression. "You were always an avid church-goer when William..." He said before realizing what he said, stopping in mid-sentence.

Mary immediately looked up when Bishop David brought up William, her knitting ceasing before she let out a sigh of disbelief escape her lips. She set the quilt and knitting needle down. "Please, do not ever bring up William to me again when comparing me to then and now." Mary said, her voice trembling as she had grown an upset expression.

Bishop David had become silent as he listened to Mary finally speak to him.

"I'm no longer the Mary from then because of the events that happened, and if you want to visit me and tell me how I use to love church and that you're concerned with me not being there on Sundays, then don't even speak, you're wasting your breath." Mary said to him, her eyes staring into his intensely.

Bishop David heard everything she was saying before he let out a sigh of sympathy. "I'm sorry Mary that you're like this...I didn't come here today to chastise you about not attending church. I came here because I'm really concerned for what you've become. I want happiness for you, I want you to have that cheerful personality that everybody knew you for." He said softly, standing up from sitting, looking down at her. "Always remember Mary, we all face events in life that we don't want, but it's all a part of God's plan for something greater."

Mary just glared at him the whole time he spoke, not even acknowledging the things he said. "I would like you to leave."

Bishop David heard her request and nodded softly, walking away from where they were at and leaving the house.

She had watched him leave through the windows before she finally reached for her knitting needles and quilt, continuing to knit as she thought about what he said about God having a plan for everyone. To her, God's plan was killing William and taking away something that she loved most in the world, when she didn't have anyone else.

"Forget God." Mary said to herself quietly, having completely lost faith and love in God.

Chapter III

One stormy night soon had arrived in Lancaster County. Rain had arrived over the town and fields, the sound of sharp pellets hitting the roofs and windows of each building. The window whirled between each building, the sounds of wind wailing could be heard by anyone who was awake.

While the storm stayed present in the county, Mary was asleep in her bed, although she wasn't sleeping soundly. The red-headed woman was having a nightmare, causing her to toss back and forth in her sleep before some sort of sound interrupted her slumber.

KNOCK KNOCK KNOCK

Mary sat right up from her bed like a vampire in a coffin, rubbing her eyes. "What on Earth?" She said to herself, looking around the room as she wondered what caused her to wake up.

KNOCK KNOCK KNOCK

This time, the red-head heard the solution to the noise. "Who could be at my door in the middle of the night?" Mary got out of her bed, wrapping her blanket around herself to cover her nightgown. She made her way down the stairs of her home before seeing the front door. Once she got to the door, she slowly opened it, seeing who it was.

There was a man, about her age, with a young daughter about six-years-old. They were wet from head to toe, shivering as they looked at Mary.

"Please...do you have room in your home for my child and I? We come from far away to Lancaster County...we have no home, no food." The man said, his tone being a desperate one.

Mary had no idea that this was what waited for her on the other side of the door. "I...Well..." She looked at the two before she finally nodded quickly, stepping out of the way.

"Oh thank you...thank you!" The man said happily and emotionally. He quickly moved inside, Mary shutting the door behind the two. Even though they were inside, away from the rain, they still were shivering in the dark home. Mary saw how cold they were and immediately knew what they needed.

She quickly went over to the fireplace in the living room, taking two logs that were on the side of the hearth in a pile and putting them inside the fireplace. After a few attempts of trying to get a fire started, she eventually managed to do so, an orange glow illuminating the living room.

Once the man saw the fire, he moved his daughter close to the fireplace, trying to get her as warm as possible. Mary saw what he was trying to do and quickly went over to the eight-year-old, wrapping her blanket around the child. The man soon began to dry off her daughter while at the same time trying to get her warm.

"There you go...nice and warm now. Away from the cold rain." He said quietly to his daughter, holding her close as he sat in front of the fireplace with her.

The daughter shivered still, but the warmth from the fire and the blanket caused the shivering to decrease as the time went by.

Mary stood behind the two, watching them and making sure that they were okay. "Are you warm enough?" She asked them, having held one of the quilts she had made in her hands to give to the man.

"Yes...thank you kind miss." He said quietly, holding his daughter close before taking the quilt from Mary, wrapping it around himself.

With the two warming themselves up from the fire, Mary decided to grab another quilt for herself before sitting down on her couch. She wrapped the quilt around her body so she could be warm too. Since she now had two "guests" in her home, she didn't want to go upstairs, back to bed, with the knowledge that two strangers were downstairs in her home, two people who she had no idea who they were.

"Maybe they're thieves," Mary thought to herself, studying the two strangers. *"Although...she looks pretty young to be a thief."* She finally decided to speak up, wanting to figure out who they were. "Where did you two come from?"

The man looked back at her, hearing her question before he began to reply to her. "We came from Somerset County." The man answered, still trying to warm up his daughter.

"Oh...that's far from here." Mary replied, sitting down on her couch, looking at the man.

"It very much is..." The man nodded, looking at her. "Do you know if there's any housing here in Lancaster County?"

Mary heard her question before she shrugged. "I'm not too sure. Are you looking for a place to stay?"

The man nodded, looking down at his daughter. She had fallen into slumber and had a warm expression on her face and had stopped shivering, indicating she was no longer freezing. "Yes."

She heard him and asked some more questions in order to get to know him. "Why Lancaster County? I'm sure there's plenty of other settlements along the way."

"I just," The man began to say, rubbing the back of his neck nervously, "I don't know...I guess I've heard a lot of great things about Lancaster. Figured that it would be a great place for my daughter to grow up in."

Mary nodded when he stated that it'd be a good place for his daughter to grow up in. "Lancaster really is a nice place to grow up in...a good place to start a fam-" she began to say before stopping when she was about to say "family." It reminded her of what she has always wanted to have and that made her think of William and her. "Well, it's a good place to meet nice and caring people."

The man saw her reaction when she was talking about family, but decided not to question it in order to remain polite. "That's good to hear...by the way," the man began to say, looking at her once again, "what is your name?"

She heard him and replied softly. "Mary...my name is Mary Lee Warner."

When the man heard her, he smiled softly. "That's a beautiful name."

Mary smiled softly when he complimented her name. "What about you? What's your name?"

"Robert." He said quietly, before looking down at his daughter, gently stroking her hair. "The little one is Miriam."

Chapter IV

The next morning had arrived, the rain was now gone, the only trace of rain being the puddles in the dirt. Mary decided to help Robert and Miriam out by going down to the church to see Bishop David could help them out.

Entering the church, there were only a few people present in the pews, praying to the Lord about whatever comes to their attention. Bishop David was not preaching, considering it was a Tuesday, so chances were he was at his home.

"Doesn't look like he's here." Mary said, turning around and leading Robert and Miriam out.

"Who are we looking for exactly?" Robert said, holding his daughter's hand as they walked towards Bishop David's house.

"We're looking for David, Lancaster County's bishop. He might be able to help you out with moving here." Mary replied, reaching the bishop's house before knocking on the door. Not too long after the knock, the door opened, Bishop David standing there.

"Mary?" He said, a little surprised. "What brings you here today?"

Mary explained the whole story to him, telling the bishop that Robert and Miriam showed up in the middle of the night, needing a place to stay and that they wanted to move to Lancaster.

"I see..." Bishop David said quietly, scratching his beard as he thought about it. "Unfortunately, there isn't any houses available right now."

Mary heard the news and let out a quiet groan. "So where will they stay if they don't have a home?"

Bishop David heard her before looking at the two, looking at Mary again. "Can I talk to you privately Mary?"

Mary was confused as to why, but nodded as she stepped inside the bishop's house. "What did you want to talk to me about?"

Bishop David looked at her before he let out a quiet sigh. "I wanted to talk to you privately about where they're going to stay. I believe they should continue living at your house until a new house can be built here in the county."

She listened to what he said before hearing his statement about the two staying at her home. "What? No. I can't have people living at my house."

Bishop David gave her a confused look. "Why not? You have one of the biggest houses here in Lancaster County. You're not living with anyone. There's plenty of room in the house for someone."

"Because, I don't have enough food to feed two more people. I don't want to start housing people." Mary was quick to say, folding her arms. "I can't let strangers come into my home and make themselves acquainted to the hou-"

"Mary." Bishop David interrupted, clearly showing he was getting irritated with her. "Enough with the excuses. I'm not going to force you to let them in. I'm only suggesting you give the two of them a home. It's not permanent, but where else are they going to go?" He asked Mary, looking at her with a serious expression. "They can't move into anyone else's home. They all have families, rather large ones too."

She listened to him, looking into his eyes as she thought about everything he was saying. Bishop David was right in many ways. Most families in the county had large families, homes that were already crowded. With Mary's house, it was just her. He even said that it wasn't permanent, so it'd be something that Mary didn't have to deal with for too long.

"I guess...I could have them stay for a little while." Mary finally admitted, realizing that she could be a little generous.

"Thank you Mary." Bishop David said before leading her back outside, now facing Robert. "We will discuss adding a house whenever I meet my colleagues. Until we can get a house added to the county, you'll have to stay with Mary for the time being."

Robert listened to what Bishop David said, nodding softly. "Okay, thank you."

Bishop David smiled softly, heading back into the house before closing the door.

Robert and Miriam turned toward Mary, looking at her. "So...are we going to back to the nice lady's house?" Miriam asked her father.

Mary heard her and couldn't help but smile. "Yes...yes you are."

Robert watched the two interact before he couldn't help but smile, seeing this stranger being so nice to his daughter.

"Alright. Let's head back to the house so I can get a room prepped up for you two." Mary said, clapping her hands together when she knew what she needed to do.

Chapter V

A couple of months passed by in Mary's household. The two strangers that had showed up on her doorstep were now friends of hers, having brightened up the household little by little. As Mary got to know Robert, he started feeling more and more comfortable around him, the two even joking around with each other.

With Miriam, she started to look up towards Mary as a mother figure, every now and then the little girl called Mary mom. Mary would hear this and laugh, finding it humorous that Robert's daughter called her mom.

While everyone was getting along just fine, Mary started to remember William again, every time she looked at Robert. There was something about Robert that reminded her of William. It might've been the way he made her laugh or the way he showed kindness to people. Whatever it was, Mary could see William through Robert, which made her think about if she found another William in her life.

It was now 6 PM and Robert and Miriam had finished eating dinner with Mary. When they finished, Robert decided to take Miriam to bed, since she started dozing off during dinner. Once she was in bed, she was out cold.

"She must've been really tired today. Miriam never goes to bed this early." Robert said, walking back into the kitchen. "I don't blame her...she didn't sleep that well last night."

"Oh poor thing." Mary said, cleaning the dishes in the sink. "I hope she rests well tonight."

"She probably will." Robert said, walking over before leaning against the counter. "So...what do you want to do?"

Mary continued to wash the dishes before she stopped, soon looking at him. "What do you mean?"

"Well I mean...Miriam is in bed early. Do you want to go out for a walk?" Robert replied, looking at her and waiting to hear an answer.

She looked at him before looking down at the dishes, thinking about his offer before setting the plates down. "I would enjoy that."

He smiled brightly before he walked out of the kitchen, planning on getting his jacket.

It didn't take long before the two were on an adventure, walking around the county in the early evening. The sky was an vibrant orange, the sun easing itself behind the hills.

"Wow...that's a beautiful sunset." Robert said softly, looking at it.

"It sure is." Mary said quietly, looking at it before she looked at Robert. With the two of them having grown closer, she soon started to think more in regards of making their relationship a bit more than friends. "Can I show you something?"

Robert heard her, turning his head and looking at her before he smiled softly. "Yeah of course."

Mary smiled brightly before leading him into the woods, walking in a certain direction. As for Robert, he wasn't sure where she was taking him, which made him a little nervous. Eventually, the two arrived in a rather large open area in the woods, a grass area that was decorated with wildflowers.

"Wow..." Robert quietly said to himself, stepping forward and starting to walk towards the flowers. "They're beautiful."

Mary stood behind Robert, watching his response before walking with him again. "I know. I love coming to this place. It reminds me of so many happy memories." She said before she began to lay down in the grass, looking at the sky that had become as orange as a Doris Longwing Butterfly's wing.

Robert watched what she did before he followed her actions, lying next to her as the two watched the sky. "You have quite the spot...especially one that you value." He smiled softly, relaxing on the grass.

The two watched the sky for a few, enjoying the time to relax with each other. Eventually, Robert spoke up, a question that had been resonating within him.

"How come you didn't want to let us live with you a few months ago?" He quietly said, still looking at the sky, some clouds gently moving along in the sky.

Mary heard him and gave him a confused look. "What do you mean?"

"You were talking to Bishop David the morning after the rainstorm. You told him that you didn't want anyone staying at the house because you didn't have enough food and didn't want housing people. Part of me though doesn't believe that."

Mary listened to what Robert was saying, her expression staying confused before her expression became more of a look of hesitant.

"There's something more than not enough food and not wanting to house people huh? You don't have to tell me, but just know I'm here if you want to talk." Robert said quietly, wanting to assure that she could trust him.

She listened to what he said before she began biting her own lip, thinking to herself before she let out a quiet sigh. "There is...there's a lot more to it. I think it's fair that you should know."

He heard her response to his question and turned onto his side, looking at her now as she began to speak about what the reason for not wanting anyone to live with her.

"It all has to do with a man I loved...a man named William." Mary said quietly.

Chapter VI

William Bradshire...a carpenter of Lancaster County. Most of the county knew him as the kind man who cared about everyone around him, even the ones who didn't care for him. William was the prime example of what it means to follow Christ's footsteps. He showed a strong love towards God, helped out around his community, showed love towards everyone, taught the youth about the Bible, and that's just the peak of the iceberg.

Sometimes in life though, bad things can occur that change one's life. For William, it was losing his parents at the age of eighteen. With his parents gone, he now owned the house, but that meant nothing to William. For a long time, he had struggled with the fact that his parents were gone, but during this time, he still continued to help people, having put them first before himself.

A great example of William putting others first was one cold, dark night. There was a knock on his door, the knock having echoed the entire silent household. When William opened his front door, he found a shivering girl his age, looking up at him. This girl was Mary.

The young girl had ran away from home, angry at her parents and her peers around her community. She was looking for a place to stay, which was she ended up on William's doorstep, a stranger to him. William was caring enough to immediately let her in; he even allowed her to stay as long as she needed. Even though she could've left any time, she found herself a priceless friendship.

Eventually, as time progressed, the redhead soon fell in love with William, the same happening with the boy. The two ended up revealing their love for each other when they discovered and rested in the grass area in the woods with the wildflowers. Ever since then, they were two peas in a pod.

As time progressed, they became closer and closer, almost being one soul. Mary began helping out in the community with him while developing a strong love of God since William introduced her to Him. Eventually, William decided that he was going to ask Mary for her hand in marriage, but his colleagues asked for his help in finishing the construction of a barn.

Unfortunately, William never had the chance to pop the question due to the accident. While he was watching his colleagues raise one of the barn walls up by pulling it up with ropes, the ropes snapped and the wall soon fell on William, his chances of escaping the wall very low with how fast the whole situation took. Sadly, William didn't survive the heavy barn wall crushing him.

Word soon got out around the county about William dying from the accident, which Mary soon heard about. She was devastated, crushed, her heart torn into pieces for the loss of her one true love.

After William had passed, Mary was given the house, considering she basically lived there and was a member of the community. During this time, Mary closed herself off from the rest of the world, locking herself away in her home, mourning the loss of William. She even decided to not let anyone into the house after the loss in order to keep the house peaceful, like it was when William and her were in it.

Even in the present, Mary still has nightmares about the whole incident, nightmares that remind her of the loss of William.

"If only I were there to stop him...to get him out of the way...If only I were there...he'd still be alive."

Chapter VII

Once Mary finished telling Robert the story, she had developed some tears from the memory of William's death.

"Now you know why I don't let anyone into the house...I know...it sounds insane, for the girlfriend of someone who has departed to keep the house like a temple. You must think I'm crazy..." Mary said quietly, wiping her tears.

"Oh no..." Robert said, looking at her. "I don't think you're insane at all...I can see why you value the house so much. All the memories with William...the laughter...the peace...everything about it...you don't want anyone to ruin this place for you." He said softly, gently resting his hand on hers. "I'm sorry...I didn't know this was the reason why you didn't want us here."

Mary heard him and finally broke down, tears rolling down her cheeks as she covered her face with her hands, muffled crying heard behind it. Robert reached for her and wrapped his arms around her, holding her close as he embraced her.

"Shhh...it's okay...Mary." Robert quietly said, stroking her hair gently to calm her down. "It's okay..."

After years of suppressing the memories of William and her, the pain she has endured from remembering his death, the many tears she had held back, she finally broke down and let her tears flow.

"I miss him so much...every day I wish I could see him again...tell him that I wish I could've saved him from the wall...I wish I could've done something." She said, pressing her face against Robert's shoulder as she shook from her crying.

"You couldn't do anything Mary...you had no idea that would happen..." Robert said softly, continuing to hold her close as she cried against him. "Look on the bright side...with William having a strong love for God, he's finally in Heaven where he can be with God...walk along with him...talk to him...laugh with him."

With Robert's words entering Mary's ears, it made her cry more. He was right in the sense that she wouldn't have known and that he's in a better place now. Her heart ached as she recalled all the memories of William from when they met to his death. All the memories were mainly happy and ones that would make her laugh whenever she looked back to them. Even though William was gone, she remembered one thing...William lives on through her. The memories, the house, the ideology, everything that William was made up of lives on through Mary. With this thought, she felt like she could finally get over the tragedy of losing William and achieve peace.

"Thank you...Robert...Thank you." Mary said quietly, looking up at him with tears in her eyes.

Robert looked down at her, confused as to why she was telling him thank you. "For what?" He laughed gently, wiping the tears away from her eyes.

"For saying all of those things about William and I...I've spent all these years holding onto William's tragedy and blaming myself for not being able to help him, but now I can finally find peace and let go of the tragedy...thank you...Robert." She finally said, looking at him as she gently reached up, stroking his cheek before she finally decided to lean in, kissing him gently.

Robert was caught off guard with the kiss, his eyebrows raising as she held her in his arms. Eventually, she broke the kiss, resting her head on his should. "Let's go back home...it's getting late." Mary said quietly, her eyes now closed.

Even though Robert had thought about pushing their relationship to another level, there was something that was holding him from reaching that level, something that had followed him from his previous home.

Chapter VIII

Many weeks had passed by since Mary told Robert about her past. Mary was in a much brighter mood, slowly building herself up again by socializing with people, going to church again, which made Bishop David happy, and she started wearing colorful clothes again.

Robert was thinking about what Mary had done in the wildflower area in the woods on the porch. He wanted to moved towards the next step, but the past was catching up with him.

"Hey!" Mary called out, coming up to the house with Miriam. "We've got dinner!"

He snapped back into reality, smiling gently when he saw the two. "Oh...that's wonderful. Looks delicious." Robert said, standing up and helping them take the food inside the house.

"I decided to cook something special for you...to thank you for helping me return back to my old self again."

Robert smiled and chuckled nervously, rubbing the back of his neck. "Oh...you don't have to do that."

"But papa," Miriam spoke out, looking at him, "look at the food! It looks delicious! At least let mom...Mary cook it for me."

Both Robert and Mary laughed at Miriam's comment, Mary picking her up and holding her.

"Okay, well if Robert doesn't want his special dinner, then I'll cook it for you." She said, walking in with the child.

"That'd be fantastic!" Miriam exclaimed happily.

Robert followed behind the two with the groceries, his expression being lost in thought as he thought about the past.

Dinner time soon arrived, everyone now seated at the table as they waited for Mary to come in with the special dinner.

"Whatever she's cooking, it smells delicious." Miriam said, excited to eat.

In a matter of minutes, Mary came out with a cooked turkey, the skin being a golden crisp.

Even though Robert wasn't asking for a special dinner, he was impressed with how the turkey came out. "Wow, looks really good Mary."

She smiled brightly, setting the plate down. "Well I'm glad you like it so much. I've got more coming out. I cooked some corn, made so mashed potatoes, have some greens." Mary explained to them as she walked back into the kitchen.

It took a few trips for her before she finally could sit down at the table with the two. "Alright, dig in." Mary said, taking her knife and fork, cutting into the turkey and scooping up a little bit of everything.

The dinner that they had all together was nice. Lots of laughter, lots of compliments, complete joy filled the room between Miriam and Mary, although Robert was most of the time quiet. After dinner, Miriam decided to go play with her doll in the living room while Mary and Robert were in the kitchen, cleaning the dishes.

While they were in there, Robert remained quiet, lost in his thoughts as he kept trying to shake it off. It didn't take too long though for Mary to see something was bothering him.

"You've been awfully quiet this evening...is there something wrong?" Mary asked him, continuing to wash the dishes.

"No." Robert said vaguely, not wanting to get into what was bothering him.

"You sure?" She said softly, looking at him. "You seem like you're thinking really hard about something."

"Don't worry about it." Robert said to her, trying to avoid explaining his thoughts.

Eventually, Mary let out a quiet sigh before setting her dish down, turning toward Robert.

"You know if something is troubling you, you can te-" Mary began to say to him.

"Drop it." Robert said harshly, looking at her for a few quick seconds before he finally set his plate down, shaking his head. "Just forget it...I'm going to bed." He said, leaving the kitchen and walking upstairs.

Mary was shocked by the way Robert reacted, considering it wasn't normal for Robert to be this way.

Miriam heard the commotion from the living room, looking at Mary. "Is papa upset about something?" She said with a concerned voice.

Mary heard Miriam and shook her head. "Don't worry about it dear. He just needs some time to himself."

Chapter IX

Robert currently laid in Mary's bed upstairs, his eyes closed as he tried sleeping. He didn't mean to snap at Mary, but considering his thoughts were getting to him, it was bound to happen. As he attempted to sleep, he soon felt something lay next to him, which interrupted his slumber. He opened his eyes and turned to look and see if it was Mary.

Of course, he was right in this situation. Mary was in her nightgown, having crawled in bed with Robert, getting cozy. Once he saw it was Mary, he returned back to his previous position, his back facing her. Still trying to avoid breaking the news to Mary, he soon felt her arms around his stomach, her body soon pressing against his back.

"What's going on with you? You're usually not like this." She said softly, resting her head against his back.

"I don't know Mary...I don't know." Robert said quietly, his eyes still closed.

"I feel like you do know Robert." Mary finally said. "I just feel like you don't want to tell me what you're thinking of."

He heard what she said, but didn't reply to it. The only thing he did was sit in silence with his eyes closed, trying to fall into slumber.

"You know I'm here if you want to tell me what's bothering you. I think it'd be healthy if you did though because you won't get any sleep with you thinking about whatever you're thinking. I know from experience." Mary quietly said, now closing her eyes as she rested her head against his back.

Robert listened to what she was saying before he let out a quiet sigh, trying to think about how he would explain his thoughts to her. Eventually, he decided to be straightforward with her.

"You know why I decided to move to Lancaster County?" He asked Mary quietly.

She merely shook her head against his back, indicating that she didn't know why he moved here. "Aside from finding a new home, no I don't."

Robert listened to what she had to say before he continued. "I left my previous home because my wife walked out on Miriam and I."

When Mary heard this, her eyes opened up and she sat up, looking down at him. "What? That's horrible! Why would she do that?"

Once Mary sat up, Robert turned so that he was laying on his back, now looking up at her. "To be honest...maybe I married the wrong person. She just...everything seemed fine to me. She was a good mother, I was a good father, we lived a happy life, but then one day..." He said before stopping, thinking back to that day before telling Mary what happened.

––––––––––––––––––––

"Sara?" He called out, looking around his home. "Where are you?

While he walked around the house, Miriam watched him, not understanding what was going on. "Papa? What's going on?"

"I can't find mom. She's gone." Robert said, his tone being a little more scared. "Maybe she left something saying where she went. Yeah...she leaves notes."

"Maybe...I'll help you try and find something" Miriam said, getting off of the couch before walking around their home, trying find anything that could lead to the mystery of where Robert's wife went.

Eventually, Miriam found a note that had fallen on the side of the bed. "Papa!" She called out. "I found a note!"

Robert immediately ran into the room, seeing the note in Miriam's hand. He took the note from her and began reading it. Although the hope he had on his expression when he found the note soon faded the more he continued to read it. In fact, he soon had become emotionless from what was written on the note.

"What does it say papa?" Miriam asked, looking up at him.

Robert finished reading the note, looking down at Miriam before folding the note in half, tucking it into his pocket. "Don't worry about it sweetheart. I think though...we need to move away from this county."

When Miriam heard this, she was completely confused. "Why? Why do we need to move?"

He heard her before he picked her up, looking around the house one last time. "Because I think we will find somewhere else that'll be better for the both of us."

"We basically left the county with nothing but the clothes on our back. I couldn't stand living in the same county as her and live in a house that we lived in together." Robert said quietly, looking at Mary as he finished explaining his story. "Would you stay in the same place if you found out your love left you and your child for someone else?"

When Mary heard this, she let out a depressed sigh. "No...I don't think I would." She said quietly. "Is that what's been on your mind today?"

Robert heard her before nodding softly. "I've been thinking about it for a long time now...I've wanted to move onto the next step in our relationship, but...I fear that something would happen again...I fear the odds of you walking out on us."

Once Robert said that, Mary spoke up in a more serious tone. "Robert...look at me."

Robert did as told and look into her eyes, seeing what she would say.

"I would never do that...ever in my life." Mary said, looking at him as she gently rested her hand on his cheek. "I wouldn't do something to hurt you and Miriam...I love you both, with all my heart." She said to him before she gently kissed him, breaking it soon after before resting her head on his chest. "You don't need to worry about me every walking out on you two...I care about you two so much that my heart aches. I wouldn't even think about walking out on you two."

When Robert heard this, he let out a relieved sigh, his arms wrapping around her and hugging her against him. "I love you so much Mary..."

"I love you too Robert..."

THE END

ROLLING HILLS

SHELLY MCDONALD

I drove by an old torn up sign that read "Sugar Grove, Pennsylvania: Population 566." I turned down two side streets and made a left on Trout Avenue before I found a beautiful yellow cottage that sat on Danbury Lane; outside I saw the lawns were freshly manicured and flower pots with garden gnomes took up the empty space. There were vines growing up the cottage and there was a small swing that sat by an old oak tree. I looked up at the sky and saw the sun beginning to set over the hills. I looked over at the neighboring farms and saw cows grazing in the fields nearby. I closed my eyes and listened to the animals chattering about. Other than that, silence filled the air.

I didn't come to this small town to find a cowboy, I came here because I lack emotion. I feel that has to do with a certain woman. Although, one could think the emotions forming inside me was the start of a new relationship. I was both anxious and excited except those feelings were about finding my birth mother. I slaved many late night hours working as a waitress at a small diner making trash for tips. I was grateful for the hard work because it prepared me for college. I aced my way through grad school and ended up landing a job at the LA Times. I was pretty much the paper boy but it was something. It was all that work that got me to where I am today. I skipped any romantic entanglements because I was determined to hunt this woman down and that is hard enough because she comes from a community that doesn't use technology. Lately, I had been feeling lonely. Most of my friends had gotten married and had children by now. I was a lost cause, I guess. I chose the thrill of a career over romance and diapers. I put off my search until recently because it made me feel weak. My only thoughts were about school and work. In order to be great, I needed to shut off my feelings. That was until I landed this job and my boss told me I'm like an onion and not in a good way. The layers are apparently thick and under ripe. He told me to take a vacation and find true emotion.

I walked through the door expecting the cottage to be full of floral arrangements, but I was welcomed by a small kitchen that was connected to the living room. The walls were painted a sky blue and trimmed in white. The pictures on the wall were of sunflowers and honeybees. I saw a small white couch and a small blue chair that faced a television set. A small table, sat between the two chairs, contained a sunflower shaped lamp. A blanket hung over the chair appeared well worn from many years of use. A small dining room table separated the two rooms. At the back of the cottage was a large bedroom. The room held a king size feather bed with all white linen, a large chest of drawers holding a large mirror. In front of the mirror were empty storage containers that were to be filled with my belongings. I glanced at the paintings that hung on the wall. Most of the paintings throughout the house were of beautiful sceneries.

My stomach started grumbling so I headed back towards the kitchen. I was scrounging through the cabinets when I noticed it had been stocked with groceries. A note hung on the fridge from the owners that my assistant had called and arranged for them. I reached for an apple and checked my email. I sent a short message to my boss before I called Rhonda and thanked her for the kind gestures.

It was almost 7 pm and that apple didn't curb my hunger so I decided to look through the contents of the kitchen. Pasta always sounded good and with all the Italian ingredients I saw I decided to whip something easy up. I pulled out some fresh basil, a few Roma tomatoes, a bunch of linguini pasta, and a splash of olive oil. She ended up making Tomato Basil Pasta. I grabbed the remote and sat down at the table and searched the movies on television. I found nothing and opted for classical music and enjoyed the melodies. It cleared my head of all that useless inner babble that seemed to cloud my mind. I was looking out the window and I saw 3 younger kids riding their bikes as an older walked behind them. The older one was reading a book as she walked. She kept stumbling because her mind was obviously in a far off land.

The next day I headed into town to stake out the local bakery. I parked across the street from the bakery. When I stepped in front of the building and took the site in I saw a historical sign that read, "Amish Bakery founded in 1848 by Tobias Hochstetler. The structure was crafted out of natural wood and the window panes had flower boxes carved into them. The word "Bakery" was crafted out of white wooden blocks and plastered on the side of the building. There were fresh flowers in the boxes and the lawn was beautifully tailored. I liked the wooden picnic tables that sat on the front lawn for those who wanted to enjoy the fresh outdoors.

However, I smelled treats baking indoors and that was where I wanted to be. I smelled various bread baking in the large cast iron ovens. Another whiff told me that stew was simmering in pots on the stove in the back. I found a small table in the back. I looked around for a plug remembering Amish had no power which meant no plugs.

I was grateful for my two battery banks or writing was going to be a drag. I was looking around when I noticed the tables each contained a simple vase with a small bouquet of fresh wildflowers sat in the center of each simple table cloth; silverware was already placed out on each table, they were neatly tucked into their napkins. The tables looked hand carved and the decoration that hung appeared homemade. A large quilt was mounted on the wall and it took my breath away. Each stitch was hand stitched by the women of this community. Each block contained a little something from its artist. The squares were beautifully stitched together into one large quilt and presented to the Hochstetler's.

I took notice that people were walking through the doors and taking seats at various tables. The female patrons were dressed in calf length dresses that were of a solid color. Some of the dresses were eggplant in color, but most blues and greens. The women I noticed wore black bonnets over a white prayer cap. They paired their outfit with a pair of black boots. I noticed the men wore light colored shirts and dark pants. They had suspenders that held their pants up. I didn't see a single speck of metal on a single person. When the men entered the bakery they removed their hats and placed them on a rack at the front of the establishment.

It was only a matter of time before the place was almost full. I couldn't figure it out but there was something strange. I finally figured it out the strange thing was called silence. I was in an extremely busy establishment and there wasn't commotion coming from the kitchen or in the dining area. Everyone appeared to be either being working as a team or speaking in hushed tones. The employee's smiles appeared genuine as they greeted each table. I was amazed at how different service was compared to back in the city where people were shouting and their children were climbing over the tables. People always complain about their food in a city.

The waiter came up to my table and greeted me as he did the others. He too was dressed in plain fashion. I looked past his clothes and right into his sea green eyes. I noticed his hair was cut into a shaggy style and his front tooth was slightly out of line. His skin held a golden hue from long hours of working in the sun. He cleared his throat reminding me that he was standing in front of me.

"Hello My name is Abram and I'll be taking your order this morning, are you ready to order?" He repeated his question.

I nervously mumbled something about a breakfast puff, a banana, and a cup of coffee; managing to keep my head averted so that he wouldn't see the color forming its way onto my cheeks. He nodded as he stepped away.

I groaned in embarrassment as I took my simple black laptop from its well-worn bag. I started writing an article on school bus safety while I waited for my order. My boss must really hate me if I'm writing articles on bus safety. Apparently, bus drivers forgot there was such a thing because there has been a rise in bus accidents. I looked over my laptop and noticed some of the other patrons spoke quietly amongst one another, but when the food came they said a word of prayer and ate in total silence.

Abram brought my meal and asked, "Is there anything else I can do for you?"

I thought of many things he could do for me but instead replied with a curt "no thank you".

I glanced back and watched him walk away. I found that the service staff never left the front of the business. They stood at a podium and waited for tables that needed to be serviced. If a patron looked up the waiter was immediately there. No food was sent back and as the patrons left they all thanked the chef in German. I learned "denki" meant thank you and was pronounced "den-gee." Every single table wished to speak with the baker. At first, it struck me as an odd gesture but soon I realized the admiration these people had for this family.

I continued returning to the bakery every day for the next few weeks. I became fast friends with Hannah the female waitress and learned that 6-year-old Mary helped prepare meals when she was not in school. I speak with Abram when he comes by my table. He often gave me his million dollar smile and a quick wave before he went into the kitchen. Sometimes he stopped and chatted with me for a moment, so today when he did she wasn't nervous or scared.

"Hello Annabelle, Have you written any new articles lately?"

"I've written a couple here and there but nothing concrete. Thank you for asking."

"I was wondering if you had any plans tomorrow. I'd like to take you on a picnic."

I noticed his cheeks turn red. Wow.

I sat there frozen in my chair for a moment. I cleared my throat before speaking.

"I'd love too," I responded shyly.

Wildflower

The next day I was busy throwing clothes around the large bedroom so it didn't strike me as odd when I glanced around; a bra hanging from the ceiling fan and a sock fell from the lamp onto the wooden floor. I sighed and decided on a new outfit instead. I drove to a local boutique and bought a pair of capris, solid lavender top, and a white cardigan sweater. "This outfit will look super cute with the white low top sneakers I brought with me," I thought to myself. I pulled my cell phone from my bag and located the GPS app. I looked for a place to eat. I finally found something couldn't find my way back. I drove around for a while and eventually lost cell reception. I accidentally turned left instead of right and went up a hill where I hoped it would loop around but, it didn't instead the road just kept winding around. I wasn't able to turn around or I would have, so I continued driving until finally, I discovered a road that led to the main road. I screamed and yelled at the stupid reception in this little town but I drove another 10 miles before my GPS finally said turn right here and your destination is on the left. I growled at my phone before parking in front of the cottage. I was way behind on schedule. Abram was due soon and may have even left his home already.

I was finishing up my final touches when I heard trotting coming from down the road. I didn't want to seem eager so I left the screen door closed and sat on the couch to read a book. I opened the blinds up so I could see as he got closer. I felt the butterflies begin to swarm in my stomach as I watched the set of American Standardbred horses climb the final hill. I saw a green wagon trailing behind two horses. It was an open two-seater wagon, and even I knew that was more for romantic social calls. The butterflies turned up a notch. I stood and fixed a few strands of hair and checked my breath. I hadn't been on many dates in my life but I had a feeling this one was going to be life altering.

Abram helped me into his wagon and asked if I felt comfortable? Of course, I wasn't, but I'd never let him know that. The seat was hard and moved when I moved. The swaying of the moving wagon caused me to grip the side. Eventually, I got used to the motion and my heart stilled. The brisk northern breeze cooled my flushed face. The fresh air was inviting and it smelled sweet and of freshly cut grass. I had noticed the handcrafted bales of straw, and I was curious about how long it takes for them to do the whole field. I was seated next to someone who would actually answer me with an honest answer.

"Hey Abram, how long do it take to make the bales of straw?"

He spoke with a smile in his voice. "It takes one man many hours hacking the tall grass with a scythe but other farmers often pitch in and help one another. Some help even when they're unable to because they are gracious and kind individuals."

Abram called those individuals God's disciples. I stared at this man in awe. He was such a kind-hearted man. I loved hearing him praise his community like he did because whether he knew it or not he was one of those disciples. His story reminded me of the weeks I sat at the bakery and watched the Hochstetler's as they prepared each dish with joy and hard work. I realized then that the Hochstetler's were also disciples of God. I took a deep breath in enjoying the smell of freshly cut straw mixed with Abram's scent. He seemed to notice my hearty attempt at enjoying the scent of the countryside but didn't notice her feeble attempt at scooting closer. Abram drew in a deep breath and agreed the air was nice. Perhaps he too smelled the countryside mixed with the scent of her instead.

"Have you worked at the dairy farm you were telling me about?" I asked curiously.

"No I haven't, I will start back again tomorrow so I won't see you again until the weekend. I only work in the bakery when work isn't available elsewhere." He stated

A few moments later we pulled into a meadow filled with Eastern Daisies, Bearded Beggar sticks, swamp lilies, Bulbous Buttercups and Black-Eye Susan's. It was full of colors. I saw reds and greens with bursts of yellow and blues. In the center of the white Elderberry and Meadow Rue sat a colorful quilt with a hand woven picnic basket on top. I looked around and saw grasshoppers jumping around and blue and yellow butterflies danced through the sky. Blue birds sat on branches twittering about. I still couldn't believe it was quiet enough to capture moments like this one.

"Oh Abram, it's beautiful!" I cried

"I'm glad you like it. I wanted to find a place where I could get to know you." He confessed.

I laced our hands together and we walked towards the quilt. I brushed my hands along the flowers. I stopped to smell a few; I fell down when a lady bug tickled my nose. I stayed there in that spot and looked up at the sky. What was I doing? I was busy falling in love and I forgot about my mission to find Ruth Hershberger. For now, I was going to enjoy this but I needed to use the weekdays to find out how to get in touch with Ruth.

I stood up and I continued to look around. I took everything in because I wanted to remember this day for the rest of my life. I saw his green buggy on the hillside, the cedar, and the pine trees swaying in the distance. I saw butterflies and dragonflies dancing through the sky. I watched the grasshoppers jump from flower the flower. A laugh escaped my mouth as I twirled around like a child. I felt like I had the world at the tip of my fingers and it's all because of Abram. He talked with me and he listened to me. He paid full attention when I spoke. He never strayed from our conversations, and he never looked bored. He filled me with happiness and he made me feel special.

I walked over to the quilt and sat beside Abram. Together we talked about our hopes and dreams. I picked up a carrot and took a bite before asking him

"Are you happy where you are in life because I feel really lost?"

"I was lost for some time but I prayed that one day I would figure out what I wanted and I found it. I want to open my own furniture store. Why do you feel lost "liebchen"? He asked.

My eyes got teary and I finally told him the truth.

"I came to Sugar Grove in search of a woman. I'm using you the history of your family's bakery as my cover up. I'm trying to locate an Amish woman named Ruth Hershberger. I have some urgent information I need to discuss with her. She may be the woman who gave birth to me."

Abram pulled me into his arms and kissed my head. I melted into his warm embrace, he held me like that until I felt him shifting his body.

Abram laid his body down beside me and looked me in the eyes before he spoke.

"I promise that I'll help you in any way that I can."

"I know you will," Annabelle said truly believing his words.

Abram and I watched the sunset together. Our fingers danced together on the quilt. There were moments of silence but they were filled with laughter. Abram always knew when my mind began wandering. He always attempted to pull me back and I was thankful for the distraction. I saw the stars form in the sky and knew my night was drawing to an end.

"Do you write books? Abram asked me curiously.

"I haven't thought writing books lately but it was a dream of mine growing up," I confessed.

"Do you make things for entertainment or just tools and furniture?" I asked

"You called me something earlier, what was it again?" I asked

"I called you liebchen" he blushed.

What does liebchen mean? I inquired

"It means my love" he spoke confidently.

"Liebchen sounds better than my love if you ask me," I admitted.

I learned he wanted to work with animals and wished one day to be a veterinarian, but he understood that he couldn't afford school. He looked at the sky and announced it was time to start heading home. The buggy ride home was silent but in a good way. The ride home Annabelle could see fireflies lighting up the sky and she could hear crickets chirping in the night. This night felt too good to be true. It felt absolutely bewitching. When they made it to her cottage they heard an owl hooting nearby. Annabelle giggled and confessed she wasn't used to such beautiful noises. She was used to horns honking, sirens blaring, and the usual city noises. She started to enjoy looking up and seeing the constellations in the sky and hearing the animals and insects talk in the night. It felt like a whole other universe out here. Abram pulled up to the little yellow cottage on Danbury Lane and walked me to the door. He looked a little nervous before he finally spoke up.

"Would you like to attend Sunday Worship with my family? It is always nice to listen to the bishop tell tales about "Herr Gott."

"Yes, I would love to join your family on Sunday." I eagerly responded.

"Perhaps you will see Ruth there." He spoke confidently.

"Perhaps I will."

Kiss Me

The week was long and brutal. I continued going to the bakery even though I knew Abram wouldn't be there. I managed to write send an article in and prayed it would hold over until I discovered the actual story I was searching for. I was glad Abram wasn't here because could focus on finding Ruth. I looked through the local phone book and found a Hershberger family lived in Sugar Grove. Their address was close by but I could feel myself cowering down. I also didn't want to march up to Ruth and say "hi might it possible that you carried a child 22 years?" I learned enough to know that the Amish were close knit and they weren't keen on outsiders meddling in their business.

I woke up early Sunday morning and took a bubble bath. I was daydreaming about spending the day with the Hochstetler's and learning about the Amish community that I didn't hear knocking on the door. I was in the middle of daydreaming when I heard a noise again. This time I drained the water and climbed out of the tub. I was putting my robe on when I heard my name being called.

"Annabelle, are you in there?" said a deep male voice.

I recognized that voice but I wasn't dressed to meet him at the door. I stood behind the closed door and answered back.

"Abram is that you?" I asked a little nervous

The last time I looked at the clock it had been 6 am. Who would be here so early?

"Yes, it is Abram are you alright?" He sounded scared.

"I just got out of the shower, I'm going to unlock the doors and go back to my room. Count to 60 and then you can come in." I said awkwardly

Abram busted out laughing and then I heard his faint counting. I ran to the back of the cottage and slammed the door closed. I grabbed my dress off of the hanger and threw it over top of me. I started pulling curlers from my hair when I heard water running in the kitchen. I was curious about that but opted to put on my shoes and fix my hair instead.

Abram helped me into the buggy. We trotted the three miles to his family farm and picked up his sisters Hannah and Mary. The girls looked a little flustered but neither said a word at first. Hannah broke the silence.

"Grosseldre and Maemm rode with Daed to the Yoder bauereie. "

Mary apologized when she interrupted her sister but she saw Annabelle's uncomfortable shifting.

"Hannah our guest doesn't speak Pennsylvania Dutch perhaps you should use Englisch."

Hannah's faced reddened before she apologized.

"Our grandparents rode with our parents to the Yoder Farm so we don't need to pick them up this morning."

"Mary that was kind of you to include Annabelle into the conversation, Herr Gott is smiling down on you for your acts of kindness." The young child's wise older brother acknowledged.

The buggy pulled onto a large farm and parked next to the other rows of wagons. The farm was beautifully maintained. She had noticed the clothes line pulley first, they were empty today. There are usually animals roaming about but today they were confined to the barn. Worship was held on that warm summer morning because there were 200 people that showed up to hear the bishop speak. After he finished speaking children began playing a game in a nearby field. Men helped with farm work as the women prepared the covered dishes. I saw the elderly in chairs and gossiping about the latest news.

The food tasted amazing but I enjoyed wandering around and meeting new people. I was so curious about their lifestyle so I excused myself to take a deeper look. I walked into the big red barn and walked past rows of cows, sheep, and horses. Occasionally I'd pick up some straw and feed an animal. She walked by a pen of baby pigs and melted. They were oinking and oinking. I left the barn and walked towards a tree covered area that separated the farm from the fields. I stumbled upon deer drinking from in a stream and fish skipping in the water. I saw spider webs with dew on them spread across some blackberry bushes. I pulled out my phone and captured the rare moments of beauty.

I was walking back to the others when I saw a woman who looked vaguely familiar. She was helping a small child fix their clothes near the outhouse. I waited until the child ran off before trying to speak with the woman. Maybe she knows Ruth or perhaps she is Ruth. There was something that was pulling me in the direction of that woman. I was about to greet her but she took one look at me and turned and walked away.

The pain felt was unimaginative. My guts hurt and I felt couldn't breathe, I looked for the only one who knew my secret.

"Abram, I am so sorry, but do you think you could take me home? I'm not feeling well." I asked teary eyed.

"I need to let my parents know but I'll meet you at the buggy." He said while walking towards his father.

Abram told his parents that he had to take me home because I was feeling ill. I looked at the row of buggies and was extremely lost. I found Abrams two horses and climbed into the buggy behind them. She was prepared to wait because she knew he was speaking with his family. I leaned forward and saw a tall gorgeous figured getting closer, so I stuck my head out and waved. He bellowed a deep laugh.

"Annabelle that's the wrong buggy Annabelle laughed so hard, but she swore those were his horses. She even fed them saved carrots from her meal.

When we got to my cottage Abram could feel I needed to talk so he asked if I'd like to take a walk. We were walking on the dirt road for a little while before he pulled me onto a walking trail. As we walked the trail Abram took my hand before speaking.

"What happened today at the Yoder farm?"

"I tried to speak to this woman who looked familiar, but she ran away."

I know it sounds childish but I believe it was Ruth.

We walked and talked for a while before Abram spotted a stream. He found a large leaf and made a bowl out of it so that we could enjoy the water. We were walking again this time he took her with confidence and kissed it. We walked for a long time before I asked,

"Are we walking to my home in LA?"

"Come we will rest before we head back to your house," Abraham laughed.

He was used to long hours of walking but he understood that she wasn't accustomed to it.

We walked into a hay field where they sat and rested while they talked. I pulled a piece of straw lose and gathered the courage to see where this relationship was going.

"Have you ever been in love?" I asked timidly

Abram smiled like he was just pondering the topic himself.

"Yes, I have been in love. This woman brightens the sky when she steps into the sunlight. She lights up a room when she walks in with a smile on her face. I hear her heart beats and my world feels absolute. She walks barefoot in the sand and has skin the color of caramel. Her eyes are the color of storm clouds on a hot summer's day. Her lips look like ripe cherries ready for tasting. Abram picked up his queen and placed her on his lap. He kissed me with more passion than I thought possible. He pulled me closer and continued dancing his tongue around in my mouth. I moaned and sank into his embrace. He held me tightly and deepened the kiss. Eventually, he pulled away and kissed my nose before he spoke again.

"Annabelle Michaels, I love you more than I ever thought possible. I'd rather die a lonely man before I'd ever give you up."

We had better start back before it gets too late. I have to work in the morning and you need to find Ruth.

Deception

The next morning I woke up feeling fresh and determined. I decided to take matters into my own hands. I am going to the Hershberger farm and meet this family. I pulled out a cookbook from the cabinet. I decided to make a chicken casserole to show respect for their family. It took me a few hours to get things together and it was almost lunch time. I loaded the rental car and drove to the address I found the other day.

I pulled up to the farm and knocked on the door. The paint was peeling from the wood and the hinges were rusted. There was a large run-down barn behind the house and there was a fenced off area on one side of the house. I knocked again and shouted a greeting. An elderly woman came to the door; she spoke little English and told me to go around back.

Annabelle walked over to the fenced area and shouted

"Hello is anyone here?"

I heard the woman talking to a man in hushed tones but the man turned and walked away, but not before I could see tension rise in his shoulders.

I took a deep breath and she walked up to the woman I saw the other day.

"Good Afternoon, I am Annabelle Michaels and I work with the LA times. I'd like to write a story on your dairy farm if that is ok with you. We want to determine if there is a large difference in the way milk is produced."

The woman chuckled before responding

"I know you came here because you want to know if you're my boppli. I know you want to know if I am your Maemm."

The woman interrupted Annabelle before she could speak. She took my arm and led me to where she was working. Together we talked and pulled weeds from her garden. She naturally chastised me when I was rushed.

"Ruth, didn't you want me for a child?" I dejectedly asked

All these questions started to form in my mind but right when I was about to ask with full confidence I looked up and I saw that golden hair that caught my eye my first day in this town.

I couldn't believe it Abram knew Ruth all along. I had to know why he didn't tell me but right now I just wanted him to know that I now know his secret.

I walked over to him and asked to speak with him alone. He said he needed to finish his shift and he would come to the cottage so we could talk.

I drove the 3 miles back to the cottage in tears, I had learned who Ruth was, and I learned Abram was manipulative and he kept things from those he loved. Neither obviously loved me or cared for me or they would have been honest from the start.

I curled up on the couch waiting to hear from the airlines. I was booking a ticket and getting out of this small town. I was watching reruns on TV when there was a faint knock on the door. I opened the door and there standing was not Abram but Ruth; her birth mother was standing right in her doorway. It was the one thing I always wanted and often dreamed of. I didn't care if I had the perfect man or the comfiest shoes. I just wanted to be accepted by the woman who gave up on me.

I invited Ruth in and listened to her tale that began 23 years ago. I learned my dad was a fisherman and my parents met when my dad delivered fish to the local market. He would often purchase jam from her mom's fruit stand and one time he bought all her jam. He stopped by each summer for three years before her mom finally grew the courage to leave her roots and locate the man that filled her soul. My mother found my father and she claimed he was the love of her life but she only had a few short months with him. She felt punished by god when they discovered he had colon cancer. Her mom had just discovered she was pregnant with Annabelle when her father told her the news. My father stayed with my mom for the first 2 months but when he died my mother was forced to live in a women's shelter until she gave birth. She put me up for adoption and when I was adopted Ruth moved back to her parents and joined the Amish church.

Ruth admitted that she never mentioned Annabelle until Abram confronted her a few weeks ago. Ruth learned Annabelle was getting impatient and wanted to meet her but Ruth was ashamed that she hid her secret for so long. That was when Ruth told her story to the community and to her husband. He knew of her relationship with Annabelle's father but he was unaware she conceived a child. Annabelle drew in a deep breath and immediately thought of Abram and how hard it must have been to confront Annabelle.

"Annabelle, Darling, do you know what your plans are? Are you playing games with Abram or are you prepared to join the church? Abram isn't going to leave his heritage, he knows what he wants. It's up to you to decide if this is the life for you."

There was a knock on the door and they both knew who it was. My thinking time was up but I was fairly sure I had my answer. I opened the door and ushered him to the swing that faced the hills.

"Abram, how long have you known about her being my mom?"

His shoulders sank then he fell to his knees. I saw tears escape his eyes, but there was no way I was going to let him get away that easily. No matter how much I loved this man, he kept something from important from the person he swore he loved.

"Liebchen, I realized the day that you mentioned your birth mother's name. I won't lie, I knew who she was, but I wanted to make sure it was the right person. I didn't want to accuse someone of something she never did. Once I discovered she was the woman you were searching for I asked her to come to you when she was ready because it's her news to share. I wasn't around then and I don't know much now. I do know that there is much she eager to tell and in time I'm sure she will. We both care deeply about you and are worried you will leave. I'm sorry I kept any information from you, I only did it out of protection."

I looked into his eyes as he faced me and I saw the same as when he told me about God's disciples. He was helping a friend in need, this friend just happened to be my mother.

I hadn't seen real emotion until I saw this man's face. It was full of emotions, guilt mixed with grief and a face stained with tears. He held onto my leg like it was the only thing holding us together. I could turn cold and run away but instead, I dropped to my knees and placed my head on his chest. All I wanted was Abram and Ruth in my life. I looked up and I kissed him hard. I fell into his arms and confessed.

"Abram Thomas Hochstetler "Ich liebe dich" than one could love one's self. I used the Dutch phrase for I love you trying to prove my devotion to his heritage. I think of you daily and I pray for your safety each night. I hold you in my heart where I've held no other. There is no way I would turn and walk away; I want to be a part of your life."

He looked at me and laughed a deep humble laugh and before I could interrupt him he took my hands in his and spoke softly.

"Annabelle Naomi Michaels Hershberger, will you marry me?"

THE WEDDING DRESS

GIGI GROSS

Chapter 1

Gabriela stared at her bank account, willing it to change. There was no way she was down to a hundred and twenty dollars. She wasn't getting paid for another three days! Even when she did get paid, a majority of it would get eaten up by her rent and groceries for that week. "Oh no," Gabriela said, laying her head on her arms. She didn't want to think about it, or look at it, or have anything to do with it. Unfortunately, when the problems are in your own life, you cannot exactly run away from them.

Gabriela wanted to call Bryan and get his support. She knew he would have all the verbal support she could want, but he wouldn't be able to loan her any money. His financial situation was just as bad as hers and he made even less money than she did. Once again, Gabby re-evaluated the idea of moving in with Bryan already. It would save them a few hundred bucks a month, and it wasn't so bad. After all, everyone was doing it.

"Maybe then, I would actually have money for a wedding dress," Gabby muttered to herself.

"Having a conversation with yourself again?" Reese asked her.

Gabby quickly minimized her bank account window. "Yes," she replied, trying to put aside her doubts to talk to her sister.

"You're starting to worry me. Turn that frown upside down!" Reese said, coming over and hugging Gabby.

Gabby couldn't help shaking her head and allowing a small smile to form on her lips. "Thanks, Reese." Reese started playing with Gabby's hair, brushing her fingers through its strands. Gabby closed her eyes and sunk into the sensation. It felt so calming to have her sister play with her hair as she had done since she was a little girl.

"Your graduation is in two weeks, isn't it?" Gabby asked, making slow conversation. Reese's hands felt so good.

"Yup! I can't believe I'm actually going to be done with high school. Then, I'm going to college, and that scholarship is seriously a blessing, don't you think?"

Gabby did her best at a nod. "Yes, I don't know how we would do it without that scholarship."

"Do you think Mom and Dad will come to my graduation?" Reese asked in a quiet voice. Gabby was glad she didn't have to look her sister full in the face as she answered.

"I don't know, Reese. Dad might not come because he thinks Mom will be there. Besides, he hasn't really been here for a while. I don't know. Mom might come."

"Do you think she'll bring her terrible boyfriend?"

"I don't know, Reese, but I want you to focus on your success, not on other people. You and only you have been the one responsible for getting yourself through high school. You have studied hard, and this is your time for a reward. I was thinking just you and me could go get ice cream at Scream Cream, maybe not that night but maybe the next if you are too busy partying."

Reese knew that Gabby's money situation was tight, but she just didn't know how tight. Gabby didn't dare let Reese in on the secret. They just needed to get through the summer then Reese would be in college, and Gabby would somehow pull together enough money for just a small wedding.

"When are you going to go dress shopping?" Reese asked after a few moments of silence.

"I don't know, Reese. I will be going soon. Don't worry. You will be invited."

"Yay! You know I am so excited for you! I'll still be able to come home for Thanksgiving or fall break to wherever you guys are, right?"

"Of course, Reese!" Gabby said, finally turning and looking her sister in the eye. "Come here." Even though Reese was eighteen, Gabby was still her big sister at twenty-five. "You will always be my baby," Gabby said, trying to make Reese sit on her lap.

"No!" Reese wailed. "I shall not! I am too old to be sitting on anyone's lap."

"Mmhmm," Gabby smiled mischievously. "I'll just tell that to your striking college boyfriend when you get him."

"Eww!" Reese said. "I'm not going to sit on anyone's lap."

Gabby laughed. "Sure, you say that now. Shall I videotape you saying it and show to you in five years? Come on, help me finish making that garlic bread."

Two days later, Gabby decided to pay a visit to Bryan. They wanted to have their wedding in the middle of August. At this point, they hadn't done anything more than decide it would be held on Bryan's family farm. That decision was based on the fact that it would be a free venue, including free flowers.

"Hey, Baby," Bryan said when Gabby dropped by at dinnertime. "I made something healthy for once. You should be proud of me."

Gabby laughed. "Of course, I'm proud of you. Reese and I rebelliously did not make a salad with our meal last night, so you are doing better than me."

"Come here," Bryan said, pulling her close. He gave her a sweet kiss. When he pulled back, Gabby smiled. This was why she was with him. He always made her feel at home. "Go ahead and sit down. I'll get you a drink in a minute," Bryan commanded.

Gabby took a seat and watched Bryan careen around the kitchen, pouring drinks, draining whole wheat pasta, and preparing their plates. When they finally sat down, Gabby took his hand and listened to Bryan pray. "Thank you, God, for this meal you have given us the resources to have. Please keep giving us all that we need. Amen."

The two began eating, and Gabby finally got up the nerve to bring up the old wedding topic. "Do you think we will even be ready to get married in August? That's only two and a half months away. I'm just worried that we won't have everything ready."

Bryan sighed, but Gabby knew that his frustration was not aimed at her. "I know it's stressful. But, we've almost gotten the rings paid for." Gabby realized at that moment that she forgotten to bring her ring payment that evening.

"Sorry!" Gabby interrupted. "I forgot my payment tonight. I'm getting paid tomorrow, though. I can just give you the money then, right?"

Bryan nodded. "That's fine. I know you're tight too. But, look, we'll have a beautiful meadow, rings, our pastor will come, and gorgeous wildflowers. Maybe we can ask guests to bring a dish. I know it's not conventional," Bryan said in response to Gabby's strange look. "But, maybe they will understand. Feeding so many people can be a few thousand dollars."

"I know," Gabby nodded. "And you paint a beautiful picture. I like the way it sounds. The problem is that. . .I really want to wear a special dress. I've always dreamed of a gorgeous white wedding dress, and I just don't know if I will be able to afford one. I don't want our wedding to just pass by like it's not anything special. I want to look beautiful for you." Gabby's voice cracked with emotion, and she looked down to avoid crying.

Bryan reached over and pat her hand. "I know that it is important to you. It's important to me that you have the wedding just how you want it. But I want you to know that whatever you choose to wear, I will love it." That was when Gabby realized that her yearning to wear such a beautiful gown might not be because she wanted Bryan to think she was beautiful. Maybe she just wanted to feel beautiful for once, not for anyone else but for herself.

Chapter 2

On Saturday, Gabby left Reese sleeping at home in bed to peruse the local flea market. She needed to get Reese a graduation present, but she also didn't have a lot of money to spend on something like that. She had no idea what she wanted to get her sister, but she knew that she liked to read. Perhaps, Gabby could find a few books at a reasonable price.

Gabby was looking at a table of books, holding a couple in her hands. The three books were only twelve dollars altogether, and Gabby thought they would be a great present for Reese right before her last free summer. Gabby looked up, and her eyes fell on a shining white dress hanging on a mannequin the next stall over. Gabby left the three books on the table and walked toward the dress as if in a trance.

Her hand reached up to stroke the fabric. Just as her fingers were going to touch the fabric, Gabby wondered if she should. She looked around to see if anyone was watching her. She saw a small, elderly woman with her eyes trained on her.

"Oh, sorry," Gabby said, stumbling into an apology. "I'm sorry. I didn't know if it was alright to touch, but it's so...pretty."

"Go ahead," the woman said in a raspy but friendly voice. "You may touch it." Her smile encouraged Gabby just the bit she needed to have the courage. She turned back to the dress and stroked it. It was soft, almost like silk. The beadwork was amazing, with little detail stitched along the folds of the fabric. The bosom was covered with exquisite beadwork, and the waist came in before flowing out in a long skirt. The train was not overwhelming but still had a presence. It was as though someone had created a wedding gown out of Gabby's imagination.

Gabby's breath caught in her throat. She didn't want to turn away from the beauty. She stealthily scanned the dress for a price tag. Of course, there was not one. That must mean that the dress was handmade and would cost even more.

"Th-thank you," Gabby said, turning away from the dress and nodding to the woman. She took a backward step away from the dress and the woman.

"Are you getting married?" the woman asked, leaning forward encouragingly.

"Yes," Gabby nodded. "But, we don't have a date yet. It will still be a few months." Finally, she shrugged her shoulders and figured she might as well ask how much the dress cost. If she didn't, she would constantly wonder. At least with a number, she could walk away from it without feeling guilty. "How much is the dress?" Gabby nodded toward the wedding dress she had been studying.

The old woman smiled and leaned back. "Oh, that dress doesn't have a price. I'm sure you noticed. It is a beautiful and priceless piece. But," the woman continued speaking before Gabby could turn away. "I will let you wear the gown for free if you promise me one thing."

"What?" Gabby whispered, unable to wait to hear her words.

"You must live out your marriage according to God's will."

"I-uh-oh," Gabby seemed unwilling to respond. "I can wear it. . .for free?"

The woman nodded. "There's a veil that goes with the dress as well, but I must have you promise that your marriage will be uplifting to God. Can you do that?"

"I promise with my whole heart," Gabby said. She couldn't control the smile that spread across her face.

The woman nodded. "Very well. God, our good Lord, will hold you to your word. Now, just give me a moment to gather the dress and package it safely. Do you have a few minutes?"

"Yes, of course!" Gabby could hardly believe her good fortune. "Do you need any help? I could help you."

"That blue bag up there on the shelf, yes, that one. That's the veil. Go ahead and get that down, will you?" Gabby strained up to reach the high shelf, took down the bag, and could not help peering into the bag to examine the veil.

"What do you think?" the woman asked, nodding at the veil.

"It's amazing," Gabby said. The woman carefully took out the veil and used the comb part to place the veil on Gabby's head. She handed Gabby a small hand-mirror, and Gabby nearly cried. She looked like a real bride, not a bride who didn't have any money. Spontaneously, Gabby reached down and hugged the old woman. "Thank you," she sobbed out. The woman patted Gabby's back.

Finally, Gabby carefully folded the veil and put it back in the bag. She then helped the woman take the dress off the mannequin and store it in a garment bag.

"I have one more thing for you," the woman said as Gabby prepared to leave. The woman pulled out a thick book. "I want you to take a look at this. This dress, you see, has a long history. It has made many brides happy on their wedding day, and they all needed it in one way or another. I encourage you to find out about their stories and write your own as well."

Gabby took the thick, leather bound book in the crook of her arm and tried to give the woman one last hug while balancing her packages. "How will I find you again?" Gabby asked.

"I'm always right here," the woman assured her. "Come back after your wedding, and I'll be waiting."

Gabby smiled, thanked the woman one more time, then hurried out of the flea market, forgetting all about Reese's graduation present. The smile could not be wiped off her face. She carefully laid the dress across her backseat and could not help but sing along with every song on the radio. The only thing left to do was try it on. When she reached home, she carried the dress inside and explained the whole story to Reese who at first felt deceived that her sister had gone wedding dress shopping without her.

"I'm going to try it on," Gabby said. "Wait until I'm in it, okay? Don't come in!" Gabby shut the door with her sister outside and changed as carefully as she could into the wedding dress. Gabby could tell the dress had had sleeves at some point. But, it was now a sleeveless dress. The hem was a little long, but Gabby knew she could fix that. Around her waist, the dress fit perfectly. Gabby tucked the veil into place then opened the door with a smile.

"Sis!" Reese said. The smile filling her face was all that Gabby needed to see. "It's perfect isn't it?"

"Yes, it is!" Reese gave Gabby a hug. "I can't believe you are actually getting married!"

"It seems real now."

"It is real," Reese said. "I know Bryan would love you in this dress. I wish he could see it now."

"I know!" Gabby laughed. "But it has to be our secret. "No words to him about it. None, do you hear me?"

Later that night, Bryan came over. He got along well with Reese, and Gabby loved that about him. After all, she might not be Reese's official guardian, but she was Reese's home ever since their parents had started their incessant bickering.

The three were playing a game of Phase 10, and Reese kept smiling randomly at Gabby. "Is something wrong with you?" Bryan asked her. "Or do you two have a cheat going on?"

Both Gabby and Reese laughed. "Nope, we're not cheating," they said in unison.

"Okay, because that denial was totally believable. Come on, I know something is up." Gabby looked at Reese. They both shrugged, but Gabby could not longer keep the news in.

"I got my wedding dress today," Gabby said.

"What?! That's amazing, Gabby. Where is it? Can I see it? Was it expensive?"

"To all of those questions, the answer is no. Besides, the groom is never supposed to see the dress before the wedding day."

"I've got an idea," Bryan said, leaning forward. "Want to get married tomorrow?"

"Sorry," Gabby shook her head. "Pastor is occupied tomorrow. Besides, I'm not ready yet."

"Aw," Bryan visibly drooped. "I guess we should probably wait until we have rings, huh?"

"That would be important!" Gabby said. She gave Bryan a playful kiss and was glad that she did not feel as desperate for a dress as she had that morning.

Chapter 3

Gabby carefully opened the book the woman had given her the day before. In the excitement of trying on the dress and spending time with Bryan, she hadn't thought about it again until she and her sister were leaving church. She hadn't told her sister about the book or how exactly she had gotten the dress, but she had told her enough to be satisfied.

The book appeared to be some sort of journal. On the pages were handwritten notes, some in cursive, some printed, and clearly not all done by the same person. Beside each handwritten note was a picture of a woman wearing the wedding dress. Gabby ran her hands over the first picture. The dress had had sleeves, just as Gabby suspected. The picture looked old, and it was worn around the edges. But it had stayed faithfully in the book. Beside it was a note.

"Teresa Daniels, age twenty-four. Married to Bertram Frantz, age twenty-four, on May 7, 1978. My parents had both died when I was five. I had been living with a family friend since then. The boy I grew up living next to asked me to marry him, but I didn't have any money for a wedding, let alone a beautiful dress. I met this wonderful young woman who loaned me a dress that she had just finished making. She told me to tell my story and live my marriage in a way that would make God pleased with me. I am determined to do just that. My adoptive parents may not have enough money to pay for a wedding, but this wedding dress shows just how much God is looking out for us."

Underneath the note was Teresa Frantz's contact information. In different handwriting was a little note that said she had died in a car accident in 2004. Gabby suddenly felt as though she was holding something very sacred. The dress was only used perhaps once a year, if that, and Gabby hungrily read through each story. Each woman had something to say about how she did not have enough money or something had befallen her. Gabby wondered why their contact information was there. Did they really want someone to talk to them? And what did they want to talk about?

Gabby pictured herself eight years from now with a few small children. She would always remember how she had gotten her wedding dress. What would she say to someone else who was going to use it? Gabby could only smile.

She selected two of the most recent weddings and decided to write to their email addresses. Her message was simple.

"Hi, my name is Gabriela. I'm going to use the wedding dress. I found your information in the book, and I was wondering if you'd like to meet and have a coffee."

Gabriela went to bed at close to two in the morning. "I am so not going to be awake for work in the morning," Gabby said. She had received her payment in her account over the weekend, and Gabby spent a little time that Monday morning paying her bills. It was just as nasty as ever. Even though she had a wedding dress now, she still would not be able to save any money after paying everything necessary. She sighed and shook her head. "It's okay," she told herself.

The workday passed well enough, but Reese was celebrating when she got home because she only had two more exams before she was officially done with school. Gabby spent some of the evening quizzing Reese before she gave herself the luxury of checking her email. She had received a reply.

"It's nice to hear from you, Gabriela. I would love to meet for coffee. How does Wednesday at lunch hour sound? Would it be possible for me to meet you at the Starbucks in Clayton?

Annabel"

Gabriela rejoiced over the email. She couldn't wait to meet this woman and unravel a bit more of the dress mystery.

When it finally came time for her Wednesday lunch hour, Gabby drove as quickly as she could to the Starbucks. She ordered and looked around for Annabel. She finally found her, and the two shook hands in a formal manner.

"I'm so glad you reached out and contacted me," Annabel said. "I wondered if anyone ever would."

Gabby smiled excitedly. "I can't believe the dress was first loaned out in 1978. It still looks so new."

"Well," Annabel surmised. "The sleeves were taken off, and I think some extra beadwork was added."

"Still," Gabby smiled. "It's like I'm wearing a little bit of history."

Annabel laughed. "Yeah, it's magical the way that woman wants to help us. It's like she can just sense the desperation in someone."

"So, what's your story?" Gabby asked, wanting to fill in the blanks Annabel's note had left.

Annabel nodded. "I was eighteen when I got the wedding dress. I know, I was young. I didn't want to get married yet, but my boyfriend had gotten me pregnant. I had just found out a few days before. I had talked to my boyfriend, and he and I decided we would just have a quiet wedding, a justice of the peace deal. I didn't want to do that, but I knew we needed to do something quickly. I didn't want to be one of those boldly pregnant brides. But I was so frustrated with the whole situation, that I had just decided I would wear an old dress. It didn't matter.

"When I saw that wedding dress, though, I couldn't help but be drawn to it. When the woman told me it was free for my use as long as I lived a godly marriage, I couldn't believe my good fortune. We had a justice of the peace wedding, but I was wearing a gorgeously beautiful wedding gown. I will never forget that woman's generosity." Annabel shook her head.

"So, it made your day magical?" Gabriela asked in excitement.

Annabel laughed aloud. "Yes, it sure did. My wedding may not have been what I had imagined it to be when I was fifteen or sixteen, but it was much better than it would have been under the circumstances. Now, I have Gracen, and she's getting close to her second birthday."

"Wow! That's so amazing."

"What's your story?" Annabel leaned forward and listened as Gabriela told her about her all the financial troubles she had had. Gabriela and Annabel continued chatting until the last possible minute.

"I really need to get back to my job," Gabby said, "Or I could lose it. That is definitely not what I need right now. Look, I really enjoyed talking to you. Maybe we could get together again, and I could meet Gracen?"

"I'd like that," Annabel said. "I'll talk to you later."

Chapter 4

Gabriela finally got a reply from the other woman she had contacted about meeting: Brianne. Brianne's story had seemed really tragic, and Gabriela couldn't wait to hear about it from the woman's lips.

After the introductions, Gabriela leaned forward for Brianne's story. "I'm really glad you wanted to talk," Brianne said. "I feel like this dress has created a secret group."

"Have you ever talked to Annabel?" Gabriela asked.

"Annabel. . .Annabel. I don't think so. Was she married after me?"

"I don't remember," Gabriela said. "But I have her number. Maybe we could all three get together or even more brides."

Brianne smiled. "I like the idea. I am definitely willing to contribute. Okay, so here's what happened to me. My problem was not so much a financial one as I read in so many stories. Instead, my problem was a big fire. About five days before the date our wedding was set, some sort of electrical malfunction sparked in our house. My family lost everything. Insurance took care of the problem financially, but the dress I had so carefully picked out months before along with my shoes and veil had been consumed by the fire. Trying to get a dress five days before a wedding is pretty much impossible.

"But, this beautiful old lady performed a miracle. She let me borrow the dress. It was much better than the dress I had originally picked. Better than that, it was ready for the wedding two days early." Brianne shook her head. "I had thought I might need to call off the wedding. I was freaking out. I couldn't even go to work I was so stressed out. I had a few burn marks from escaping the house, but the dress covered them nicely. They can't even be seen in the photos."

"Wow!" Gabby said, soaking in her new friend's story. "Wow." She was silent for a few minutes as Brianne's story sunk in. "Did you know that there have been thirty-three weddings in that dress? I'll be number thirty-four."

"When is your wedding?" Brianne asked.

"It'll be mid-August, right after my sister moves into her college dorm. She's been living with me."

"Would you mind if I rudely invited myself to your wedding?" Brianne smiled.

Gabby laughed. "Of course not. You are welcome. It's going to be a small wedding, and we ask that each guest bring a dish of food, a sort of potluck. We really don't have the money for much more, but I would be honored for you to come."

After meeting the two brides, Gabby wanted to meet more. She kept setting up even more appointments with brides. She had one last meeting planned before her wedding. This meeting took a few weeks to set up. By the time Gabby met her, it was the first day of August.

"What's your story?" Gabby asked impatiently. The question had become one of which she could not wait to ask each new woman. Hallie had been married almost ten years ago.

"My story's probably a bit different from some others," Hallie shook her head. Gabby had agreed to come to her house because Hallie had three young children. Hallie wanted them to be able to play and stay out of their hair while the two women talked. "I was poor. I couldn't buy a wedding dress. That much is as normal as for any of us women."

Gabby nodded, anticipating more.

"My story becomes interesting after I married Mark. Did the lady have you make a promise?"

Gabby nodded. "Yes, I promised that I would live my marriage according to God's will."

Hallie accepted Gabby's words. "Yes, I promised the same thing. At the time, I promised it because it seemed such an easy exchange for the dress. But it wasn't as easy as I thought it would be. The first year of marriage was so difficult. I looked back on the innocence I sported on my wedding day, and I would shake my head. How had I thought I loved Mark?" Hallie was quiet as she remembered. "I was sure that we were going to get a divorce. You see, his family lives on the other side of the country. I know he was really close to them, but he agreed that living here would be the best solution for us.

"But, it was like he had forgotten that. We argued almost every night. I started to hate him. He made me cry so much." Hallie shook her head, and Gabby should see the tears brimming in her eyes. "I started fantasizing about running away and going a place where he wouldn't find me. Then, I remembered my promise. I tried to weasel my way out of it, saying that the fighting was Mark's fault. I blamed him, but I knew I needed to take credit for my part. So, I started serving Mark instead of myself.

"Even when I was tired, I would make dinner. I would clean up without complaint. He noticed after a month, and I felt him become more tender toward me. We were finally able to talk through what had been happening. That was the best day of my life, the day that we finally talked it all through without screaming. I finally slept next to him and felt connected to him again.

"Gabby, that promise is going to be hard to keep. You will probably get angry with your fiance sometimes, but don't walk away. The weak walk away; it's the strong that keep fighting."

Gabby hugged Hallie as a few tears spilled over. "Thank you, Hallie. I needed to hear those words. They were just what I needed." Before Gabby left Hallie's house, she invited her to her wedding. "I know it is only two weeks, but if you think you can come, I would really like it. Don't be shy about bringing your husband and children."

Chapter 5

On the day of her wedding, Gabby carefully donned the dress. It was to be a simple ceremony. Only her sister would stand beside her. Bryan was having his best friend stand beside him. At that moment nothing felt simple about Gabby as she waited for Reese to calmly do up the back.

"I can't believe it's really the day," Gabby said.

Reese smiled. "Yeah, I'm pretty sure I'm having the most exciting first weekend home from college out of all of my friends." Of course, her statement made Gabby start asking about all of Reese's new friends. She had to make sure that her baby sister was doing well and having fun in college.

"Is it done?" Gabby asked.

Reese nodded. "It's done. You're all ready."

"Well, not completely," Gabby said. "I look fine, but I feel a bit nervous about walking down that aisle."

"Why?" Reese asked. "Are you unsure about Bryan?"

"No," Gabby shook her head. "I know he is perfect for me, well, as perfect a fit as someone can be with my rather strange personality."

Reese laughed. "Then, what is making you nervous?"

"I guess it just hit me that this is a lifelong commitment. I love Bryan, and I just don't want anything to go wrong. What if we start living together, and he does annoying things that get on my nerves?"

"Like what?"

"Like leave his socks on the bed."

"Then tell him to take his socks off," Reese shrugged. "It's not that hard. Look, if you love him and you know that for sure, then you just have to go through the bad stuff and remember that. Then you'll get to the good times, and it'll be all worth it."

"Alright, my sister the wise," Gabby smiled. "What time is it?"

Reese looked at her phone. "We still have thirty minutes."

"What a long thirty minutes that'll be!" Gabby sighed, carefully sitting in her dress.

Reese laughed aloud. "I thought you just said you were nervous to do it, and now you can't wait to go down the aisle."

Gabriela laughed with her sister. "When you get to this point, I will be right by your side and remind you of everything you just said. Meanwhile, you'll just be like. No, I'm nervous! Let me be nervous by myself!"

Gabriela's friend Erica burst into the bedroom just then. "Hey! Wow, Gabby! You look so amazing!" Erica was the unofficial photographer. She had a professional camera and had done some photo shoots. A free photographer was her wedding gift to her friend. "Look, we don't have a lot of time, but I wanted to get a few pictures of just you in all your bridal beauty, then maybe a few with Reese. Hey, Reese! How are you?" Erica said in one breath.

Gabby laughed. "Oh, Erica, I knew there was a good reason we were friends." Erica took all the photos she wanted with Gabby sitting, standing, lounging, smiling, and serious.

"Alright, Reese, get in there with your sister." After a few more shots, Erica hovered over to the door. "Alright, I believe we have five minutes before your little flower girl will start her march. Let's get you safely down these stairs."

Gabby carefully maneuvered the stairs with the help of her sister and friend. The stairs were not very wide and definitely not prepared to have brides tramping up and down them. She finally stood by the back doors.

"Ready?" Reese asked.

Because Gabby had decided against having their estranged father walking her down the aisle, Reese would be walking right beside her.

"I think so," Gabby answered. "But ask me again in a minute, and I might have a different answer."

"You've got this, Sis."

"Thanks."

Erica reappeared as the music started to assist the flower girl on her way. Next went the ringbearer. After that came Gabby and Reese. It was a simple, small wedding, just as Gabby had dreamed it. Best of all was Bryan's face when she came through the doors of the back of the farmhouse.

His smile was genuine and delighted, and Gabby looked only at him as Reese guided her steps down the aisle. When she reached the altar, she placed her hands in Bryan's, smiling into his eyes and wondering how she had ever doubted her decision to marry him.

"I love you," she whispered as the pastor was talking to them. He mouthed the words back and gave her hands a squeeze. Suddenly, the ceremony, including a candle lighting, a song sung by a friend, and a short talk from the pastor seemed all too long to Gabby. After what seemed an eternity, the words she had wanted to hear for so long pierced her thoughts.

"You may now kiss the bride."

Gabby kissed Bryan, leaning into his lips. When they pulled back, Gabby felt the magic of the moment lingering. "You're my husband," she whispered, incredulous.

"And you, my dear, are my wife." Bryan let go of one of her hands, facing the audience. The pastor announced them, and Bryan paused before they started down the aisle. "This is my wife!" he shouted, his pleasure clear as he lifted up their joined hands in victory. Gabby started laughing. Suddenly, a huge cheer rose up from the back of the rows of seats. Gabby looked over and counted five of the former brides that she had met.

"Yes, Gabriela!" They screamed together. While Gabby had not pictured her wedding as loud as a ballgame, she couldn't help laughing aloud.

Bryan carefully led her down the steps, and they entered the old farmhouse. As soon as they were inside, Bryan turned to her and kissed her passionately. "You are the most beautiful bride I have ever seen," he whispered. "And tonight, I will make you mine." Gabby trembled with anticipation, leaning in for another kiss.

A week later, Gabby carefully zipped the wedding dress into the garment bag for the last time. She took out the book and carefully glued in a photo of herself wearing the dress. She smiled at the photo then took up a pen and began writing in her best cursive beside the photo.

"Gabriela Winfox, age twenty-five. Married to Bryan Davis on August 21, 2016. This dress changed my life. Not only did it give me a chance to have the kind of wedding I would never have had on my budget, but it showed me the friendliness and generosity this kind of world doesn't see very often. It made me promise to be a more generous person and to look for opportunities to help others. I didn't have any money for a nice wedding, and my fiance and I feared we would not be able to throw a wedding. Determined to get married, because we knew it was right, I thought I would never have a wedding dress. I was wrong. Please, contact me. I would love to talk to you, and I know that the brides I met would love to talk to you as well. We are in this together."

Gabriela signed her name under her words and closed the book with a solemn thud. "Thank you, God," she said as she loaded the dress, veil, and book into the back of her car. She was on her way to the flea market.

HUMBLE
SAMANTHA COLLIER

The smell of bumbleberry pie, fresh from the wood oven, wafted through the house from where it was cooling on the window ledge. Lizzie's stomach rumbled as she made her way to the kitchen.

Her mother had baked it especially, as they were expecting visitors. Lizzie's dear friend Gloria and her mother should be here any minute.

"Lizzie! Go and change that apron," her mother said to her now. "It's covered in purple juice."

Lizzie looked down at her apron. It *was* a little stained with berries. Just as she was contemplating it, the sound of a buggy pulling up distracted both of them.

"They're here!"

Lizzie ran down the steps to welcome them.

Gloria smiled when she was her friend bounding down the steps. Dear Lizzie. Such a gentle soul. It was wonderful to see her happy and smiling. It didn't happen very often.

Within minutes, the visitors were sitting at the kitchen table. The bumbleberry pie, full of Lizzie's freshly picked berries, had been cut into slices and put on plates. A pot of coffee was ready to serve.

"Mrs Hertzler, this is wonderful," Gloria said as she took a mouthful of pie.

Gloria's mother, Mrs Schwartz, nodded assent.

Mrs Hertzler waved a hand in dismissal. "You are both too kind! Just something I whipped up quickly. There are so many berries this summer, I can't seem to keep up with them. Lizzie picks them daily."

"Lizzie, some things never change!" Gloria remarked to her friend. "You always have loved wandering by yourself, hunting and gathering. In fall, its mushrooms, in summer it's the berries."

Lizzie laughed. "I like being in nature, you know that. I feel more alive when I am wandering in the fields. You can see all the birds and wildlife. Being cooped up in the house drives me crazy."

Gloria put down her fork. "*Ja*, you have always loved it," she agreed. "Which leads me to why I have come to visit today." She took a deep breath, then turned to her friend.

"A group of us are going camping next week," Gloria continued. "We want to go to the lake to the west. The boys will go fishing, of course, but there will be other activities. A lot of us want to go bird watching, which I know you love. It's such a beautiful summer, we have to make the most of it!"

Lizzie looked down at her plate. "Thank you for the offer, Gloria, but I really can't. Mammi needs me here, don't you Mammi?" She looked at her mother pleadingly.

There was an awkward silence. Mrs Hertzler shifted uncomfortably on her seat.

"Lizzie," she said eventually. "I can spare you for a few days. It would be good for you to socialize with the young people." She looked at Lizzie. "I think you should go."

"But, Mammi..." Lizzie trailed off. She didn't know what other excuses to make. Why couldn't her mother back her up? She, more than anyone, should know why Lizzie couldn't go on a camping trip. It was out of the question.

"Lizzie, think about it," Gloria said. She looked at her friend. "I think it would be good for you. We want you to come."

Lizzie hung her head. "I will think about it," she answered eventually.

"Good!" Gloria picked up her fork. "Now, let's finish this pie before it gets cold."

***

After the visitors had left, Lizzie turned to her mother as they were clearing up.

"Mammi, I can't go," she said. "You know why."

Mrs Hertzler looked at her daughter. "I do know why." She took a deep breath. "Which is why I think you must. Lizzie, you need to make peace with it. I think it would be good for you. You live too much in the past, my *lieb*."

Lizzie felt tears pricking behind her eyes. "I try! You know I do. But it is so painful."

Mrs Hertzler put down the plate she had picked up and took her daughter's hand. "It is painful for all of us," she said softly. "But it is *gelassenheit* –you need to submit to God's will. We have to let it be and move on with our lives."

Lizzie slowly nodded her head. "I will go if you insist. But I will never make peace with it."

Mrs Hertzler sighed. "Making peace and letting go doesn't mean we forget," she said.

She picked up the plate and walked to the kitchen.

Lizzie stared after her mother. She knew, in her mind, that her mother was right.

It was her heart that couldn't move on. Her heart, that always ached with the memory. That kept her awake at nights, soaking her pillow in tears.

Her heart couldn't let it be. She knew that God didn't like it when you couldn't accept what his plan was for life. She had prayed and prayed for guidance, but still, every day was full of the memories. Which is why she liked to wonder so much by herself outdoors. It was the only place her heart could rest - for a little while, at least.

Her mind drifted back to that awful day, as it had so many times over the years...

It had been a hot summer, just like this one.

She had been nine years old.

Her family had gone on their annual camping trip. She remembered the joy of packing and departing for it. She had packed her sketch book, so she could draw all the birds and insects they would discover. She had always loved being in nature.

The first few days had been wonderful. They had fished, and bird watched. Lizzie had run barefoot and happy through the fields.

On the fourth day, her little brother Stephen had pestered her parents and other siblings to take him swimming, but everyone was busy.

Eventually Lizzie had said yes, and led him down to the creek.

"Don't stray too far," her father had called out. "Stay where we can see you. The creek has a current. Not too far out."

They had happily swum where they could be seen for a while, but then Stephen had gotten restless.

"Let's go further up," he had said to her.

"No, Stephen," she said. "It's not safe, you know that."

But her little brother had already started swimming away. She called to him, but he ignored her.

She had no choice but to follow him.

She knew he was in difficulty when she could see his head ducking under the water for longer periods. But she couldn't seem to get to him quick enough.

His arms were raising in the air. She could hear him coughing, spluttering water as his head ducked under. She swam faster, calling out to him.

"Stephen! Try to get to the other side, grab the branch," she screamed.

Her last vision of him was his blonde hair slipping under the water.

Then he was gone.

"Stephen!" She screamed his name over and over. But there was no response.

Her shouts had brought her father, who was in the water now, swimming frantically to them.

They searched and searched.

But it was all too late.

They eventually found him washed against the bank.

He was dead.

He had been six years old.

Lizzie leaned against the kitchen table as the memory flooded through her.

It was her fault. She had been trusted to take care of him, and she had failed. It didn't matter that her parents had been gentle with her, and had never blamed her. She knew. It had burnt a hole in her heart, a hole that seemed to get bigger with each passing day.

She could never forget.

The thought of going camping again made her heart beat faster. Why was her mother insisting? It was too painful. It didn't matter where they went, the memories of her last camping trip would be forever imprinted over it. The mere thought of it made her head spin.

It is gelassenheit – you need to submit to God's will.

Her mother's voice echoed in her brain.

She knew God worked in mysterious ways. She knew He always had a plan.

She needed to trust in that. If she prayed more, maybe she would finally see the truth.

***

Lizzie packed with trembling hands. She remembered the joy she had felt when she had packed for that long ago camping trip. This time, there was nothing but dread.

She had wavered over the course of the week. One minute she said she would go, the next she declared that it was impossible. Eventually her father had sat her down.

"Lizzie," he said. "I think it is important that you go. I know you are fighting it, but I think it will be good for you. You have to move on. We will never forget Stephen, but you are our child as well. We worry about you. We want you to live your life and follow whatever path our Lord has chosen for you. You can't do that when you live in the past."

Lizzie embraced her father. "I will try, Daed," she whispered.

Which is why she was here now, buttoning up her bag.

"They're here!" Her mother's voice drifted up the stairs to her room.

Lizzie took a deep breath, picked up her bag and ran down.

There was a convoy of three buggies. Gloria jumped down from the first, her face beaming.

"Oh, Lizzie, I am so glad you decided to come!" She hugged her friend, helping her into the buggy.

Waving to her parents, Lizzie settled in. It was only then that she looked at who was driving the buggy.

It took all her strength to stop climbing back down and insisting that she had changed her mind.

"Lizzie, you remember Elam, don't you?" Gloria said. "He was at school with us."

The blonde young man with the ice blue eyes turned towards her. He smiled.

"Lizzie," he said. "It has been so long."

Lizzie forced a smile onto her face. "*Ja*, it has," she answered. Why did her voice sound so shaky and tremulous?

The smile froze on Lizzie's face. Her heart started to beat faster.

Of all the people in the world. It had to be him. Her old school yard crush. Elam Blauch.

She hadn't seen him in years. She had almost forgotten all about him.

Hadn't she?

As the buggy cantered on, Lizzie reflected that it wasn't true – Elam had stayed as a burning image in her mind, always.

***

They set up camp in the early afternoon.

Lizzie wondered off by herself after she had helped. She felt awkward – she wasn't used to being around a group of young people anymore. Probably the last time she had was when she had been at school.

School. She shuddered at the thought. She had never enjoyed it, after what had happened - she felt everyone's eyes on her. She could almost hear them whispering about her – about how she had let her little brother drown.

It was safer, on her own.

The walk was pretty, and she was collecting a small bunch of wildflowers when she heard a twig snapping behind her.

She turned. Oh, no. It was Elam!

He saw her, and smiled.

"Lizzie," he said. "I saw you wander off by yourself. I thought you might like some company."

Her mouth had gone dry just looking at him.

"Did you? Well, I don't really," she answered quickly, then could have kicked herself. How could she be so rude? Her mother would have frowned if she had have heard.

Elam looked surprised. "Alright, I will leave you then," he said, and turned and walked away.

Lizzie watched him leave. She was glad, wasn't she?

But she didn't feel glad. She felt bereft, like something vital had been torn from her.

She kicked a stone, stubbing her big toe in the process. She didn't understand anything, anymore. She should never have come on this stupid trip; she was angry with herself for being talked into it.

There were the memories of Stephen, of course. But there was also Elam – she never would have agreed if she had have known he was coming.

The humiliation of that day in the school yard had never left her, either...

It wasn't long after Stephen's drowning.

She had stayed away from school for a while. But when she returned, she felt like the girls were whispering behind her back. She felt like everyone's eyes were on her, judging her.

They had gone to play a game of baseball on the field, something she hated. She always fumbled the ball and could never throw far enough.

She dragged her feet as they walked there, and stood awkwardly until it was her turn to bat. She kept missing the ball. Were people snickering at her clumsiness?

Elam wasn't, she knew that. He was the only one who encouraged her. "Good try!" he would call.

She hit the ball! It sailed away over the field, and she ran to the base like her life depended on it. She could hear Elam clapping her.

Mary Miller noticed, too.

"Elam Blauch likes Lizzie Hertzler!" she sang out. Everyone laughed. Elam colored and looked at the ground.

Lizzie wanted to die. It was hard enough to be here, walking and talking like normal, after what had happened. To be the centre of attention like this was too much.

She simply walked away, back to the school room. "Elizabeth Hertzler!" Miss Umble, her teacher, had called after her, but she kept walking.

She knew she would be in trouble. She was defying her teacher. She couldn't do anything right!

But she never forgot Elam's kindness to her that day.

He became her secret crush. Her eyes would follow him wherever he went. But she knew he didn't like her, after the baseball game. After all, he had been humiliated, too.

She had left school a few years later. And she hadn't seen him since. Until now.

***

The men had wondered to the lake with their fishing rods by the time she got back to the camp.

Gloria was sitting with three other girls on the ground near the tents, but stood up when she saw Lizzie. "Come sit with us," she called. Lizzie had no choice – she had to go and sit with them.

The other girls made room for her. She had gone to school with all of them, but they had never been great friends. Lizzie was disconcerted to see Mary Miller, her school yard tormentor, among them.

"Where did you wander off to?" Gloria asked, a puzzled smile on her face. "We were starting to worry!"

Lizzie looked at her friend. "Just picking these," she said, handing the flowers to her friend.

"How sweet," Mary drawled. Gloria looked at her sharply.

"There is nothing wrong with wildflowers, Mary," she said.

Mary raised an eyebrow. "Whatever you like, Gloria." She sniffed, looking around at the group. "It is so hot here! Who wants to go for a swim?"

The girls all nodded enthusiastically. All except Lizzie.

"You all go," she said quickly. "I will mind the camp."

"As you please," said Mary dismissively.

The girls rose and changed into their bathing costumes, gathering their towels.

Gloria came up to where Lizzie still sat. "Are you sure you'll be okay?" she asked.

Lizzie nodded her head. "Of course! Enjoy."

She watched them go.

The thought of swimming sent chills through her, even though it was a hot summer's day.

She should never have come. She just wasn't good in groups. She felt a thousand times lonelier in a group than when she was in her own company.

How she wished she had never let her parents talk her into it.

***

That night, in her tent, she could hear people whispering and giggling. She curled up in her sleeping bag tighter, even though it was so hot even a sheet would have felt like a heavy blanket.

They had feasted on the fish the men had caught, then told stories before retiring. It was strange, but Lizzie felt like Elam was watching her the whole time. Yet when she turned towards him, he quickly looked away, so she was never sure if she had imagined it or not.

He was probably looking at Mary, anyway, who sat just beyond her. Mary, with her dimples and her sweet dark eyes. She had always been popular with the boys, and she knew it. She would simper after them like a little puppy dog whenever they talked to her.

That wasn't a very charitable thought, Lizzie chided herself. She shouldn't be resentful just because Mary was pretty and she wasn't. We all have our gifts, thought Lizzie. She just couldn't think of any that she had, that might make a man think she would one day make a good wife.

She wasn't a great cook, like her mother. She didn't quilt beautifully, like her sisters. She was clumsy and broke things when she was inside. The only time she felt good about herself was when she was roaming the fields.

Restlessly, Lizzie turned over in the sleeping bag.

Elam. She had not allowed herself to think of him in so long. And now here he was, as handsome as ever. And as kind. He had grown taller than she imagined. It seemed forever since the school yard days, when she had watched him covertly.

Why did he make her so tongue tied? Why did she blush so furiously whenever she was near him?

It didn't matter, anyway. After her rudeness to him today, he would probably never want to speak to her again.

***

She was picking random wildflowers again as she wondered through the woods the next day.

Many of them were the same as the ones that grew around her family's property, but there were many that were different. She hadn't seen the gentle mauve petals of the wild bleeding heart around home, nor the fiery red beauty of the Indian blanket flower.

Absorbed, she was so intent on the flowers she didn't notice Elam, crouched in the shrub, until she almost stumbled over him!

He jerked in surprise. "What are you doing here?"

"What are *you* doing here?" She repeated his question back without thinking. Of all the people to stumble into in the woods!

"I am bird watching," he said, his voice a whisper. "I have my eye on a bird, in the tree just beyond." He pointed to where he meant.

Without thinking, Lizzie crouched down next to him, shielding her eyes from the blaze of the sun.

"I think I see where you mean," she whispered, squinting. He looked at her for a moment, then handed her his binoculars. She took them absently.

"Yes!" she hissed, peering through them. "There he is! I can see him clearly!"

"I thought so," said Elam excitedly. "I was so sure I heard his call. I've been on his trail all morning."

"I think it is a lazuli bunting," breathed Lizzie, putting down the binoculars. "Do you know how rare it is to spot him?" Her eyes were glowing.

Suddenly, she became conscious of how close she was to Elam.

She turned slightly, toward him. He turned toward her at the same moment.

Their eyes met and locked.

Lizzie felt a shuddering all the way through her, from the top of her head to the tips of her toes. His eyes were the clearest ice blue she had ever seen. She felt like she was drowning in their depths.

What was happening to her?

Confused, she turned away, breathing heavily.

"So you like bird watching?" Elam spoke in a ragged voice. His breathing sounded as heavy as hers.

"*Ja*," she managed to answer. "It is one of my favorite things to do in the world."

"Mine, as well," he said.

They were still crouched close to each other, so close she could see the light stubble on his chin and the angles of his chiselled face.

"Lizzie..." he breathed.

She jumped to her feet, startling him.

"I must apologise for my rudeness yesterday," she said, brushing twigs off her dress. "It was so unnecessary."

"It's okay," Elam answered, standing up himself as he looked at her. "I startled you. You were enjoying a walk by yourself. I understand – I like to have time to think as I walk by myself, as well."

"You do?" she asked.

He nodded his head. "I think we are very alike." He turned to look at her intently. "We both love being in nature. I feel so much more alive when I am outside, discovering animals and plants."

"So do I," she breathed. "I thought I was the only one! Everyone always makes fun of me for it, like I am so odd. They don't understand my need to be outside."

They smiled at each other, as if they had just shared a big secret.

"Maybe I am as odd as you," he said.

Lizzie stared at him. Was he as odd as her? Had she met someone who finally understood her?

Was it possible? Her heart started to expand, just a little.

***

They walked back to the camp later that morning, still talking excitedly about the lazuli bunting they had seen and the other life in the forest.

"Did you see that white- tailed deer running through the shrub?" Elam was saying. "She was small, but I am sure she had a fawn next to her."

"*Ja*," Lizzie answered. "She did! They were so far off, it was hard to tell, but I am almost sure I spotted two."

"God's creatures are marvellous," he said.

"I would have loved to have been on the Ark," Lizzie mused, smiling. "I used to imagine it when I was little, being surrounded by all of God's creatures."

"So did I!" Elam turned and smiled at her. She smiled back, her heart full of happiness.

"Where have you two been?"

They jumped at the voice. It was Mary Miller, standing there with her hands on her hips.

"Just bird watching," Elam answered.

Lizzie felt her spirits deflate. She had never liked Mary. Did she tilt her chin when she spoke to Elam, tossing back her shoulders? And did Elam square his as he looked at her?

It was no use. Girls like Mary always ended up with the boys. How many times, when she had been forced to attend Evening Sings, had she seen it happen?

Elam wasn't interested in her. When the time came, Elam would choose a girl like Mary to be his wife. Although he had a lot in common with Lizzie, she would be more like a friend – one of the guys. She never stood a chance.

She walked away without speaking, not noticing Elam's intense stare after her as she left.

***

Voices rose in the summer night air, filling it with sweet harmonies.

After dinner that night, they decided to sing. Mary led it. She had always been a leader.

Lizzie sat with the group, mouthing the words to each song.

She remembered clearly when she had loved singing, prior to Stephen's passing. It had filled her with joy. Now, it was like most other things – something she had to do.

She watched Elam singing with all his heart. He had a wonderful voice – deep, full of devotion. She felt she could sit and listen to him until daybreak.

Amazing Grace, how sweet the sound
That saved a wretch like me!

Lizzie jolted out of her reverie. Oh, no! Not *Amazing Grace*. She didn't think she could endure it.

She stood up, leaving the group to wonder off into the night. She could feel everyone watching her. Let them watch, she thought fiercely. I don't care anymore.

She rested her head against a black maple tree, feeling the bark rough and cool against her face.

"Are you alright?"

She turned. Elam was standing there, watching her.

She forced a smile. "*Ja*, I just felt a little hot," she answered, with difficulty. "I thought it might cool me off, if I took a walk."

"Don't you like *Amazing Grace*?" His face was still as he looked at her.

Why was he pestering her? Why couldn't he just let her be?

She looked up into the sky. The night was inky black, with tiny pinpricks of light from the stars.

"It is a beautiful song," she said, slowly. "It is just difficult for me to hear it. It reminds me..." she trailed off. A lump had formed in her throat.

"Reminds you of what, Lizzie?" His voice was gentle, almost lulling. Why did she feel like burying her head in his chest when she heard it?

She took a deep breath. "It was sung at my little brother's funeral," she stated. There! He had got it out of her. Was he happy?

He didn't look happy. He stepped closer to her, taking her hand. His skin burnt against her own.

"*Ja*, I can see why it would be difficult," he said. He looked down at her.

She could barely see him in the darkness, but she felt him all around her. His concern for her. His kindness. And something else, that made her tremble inside.

He pulled her closer. She was falling against him. It felt natural as breathing...

What was she doing? She came to her senses with a jolt, stepping away from him.

He smiled, gently. "We can stay here, until you feel ready to join the group." He glanced around. "The cicadas are threatening to drown out the singing, anyway!"

She laughed. Indeed, the cicadas had started, their high-pitched calls overtaking the night air.

"I am ready," she said.

They turned and walked back to the group. Lizzie felt lighter; it was like he had untangled a small knot inside of her.

***

The next day, the sun was rising higher in the sky. It was so hot Lizzie felt sweat trickling down her neck, from the line where her *kapps* met her hair.

"We have to go swimming again!" Gloria was fanning herself with a leaflet. "It is too hot to think!"

All the girls nodded. The boys had already had the same idea, and left for the lake half an hour before.

"Lizzie, you must come today," Gloria said, looking at her. "You look so hot I am afraid you might melt."

"I am fine," Lizzie answered quickly.

"Oh come on, are you scared?" It was Mary, chiding her as always.

Lizzie lifted her chin a little. "I just don't enjoy swimming," she answered.

"Well, walk with us down to the bank, at least," Gloria said. "You can wet your feet if you don't want to swim. That will cool you off a little."

Lizzie hesitated. What harm could it do? She could sit on the bank and look at the lake.

"Alright," she said.

The girls jumped straight in as soon as they got there.

Lizzie sat down, staring out at the ripples on the surface of the lake. It was so beautiful. She could see the men swimming a bit further up, splashing and dunking each other. They looked like they were enjoying themselves.

She spotted Elam, his blonde hair slicked back with wetness. The water glistened on his arms and face in the sun.

Her breath caught. She had to look away. Why was she so mesmerised by him?

"Lizzie!" Gloria waved to her from where she was swimming. "Come and dip your feet!"

Lizzie shook her head, trying to smile, to take the sting out of her refusal.

"Lizzie, you are such a baby!" Mary called.

Everyone was looking at her, laughing. She knew they thought she was odd, and whispered about her.

And Mary Miller had called her a baby.

Resolutely, she stood, approaching the waters' edge. She waded in a little, feeling the coolness of it on her hot skin. It felt refreshing.

Suddenly, she was being pulled in. She hadn't seen Mary approaching her until the girl's arms were dragging her into the water.

"No!" she screamed, resisting. Mary laughed.

She fought, but Mary was stronger. She suddenly lost her footing, and plunged into the water, face first.

She gasped, clawing to get to the surface.

She could hear Stephen's cries, his desperate attempts to remain above water.

Her own voice, calling to him, pleading with him to stay safe.

She was choking. The water was claiming her, just like it had claimed him. She felt it pulling her under, slowly, slowly...

Strong arms were around her, dragging her above the water. And a gentle voice, crooning to her, whispering into her hair, "It's alright. It's alright. I've got you."

She opened her eyes.

It was Elam, pulling her to safety. She rested her head on his chest in relief. She could feel the soft thud of his heartbeat.

He lowered her down onto the bank, his blue eyes full of concern.

"Lizzie, you are safe," he whispered. He stroked her face gently.

She stared up at him. The sun was behind him, so he looked in shadow. Even so, she didn't think she had ever seen anything more beautiful in her life.

She loved him.

The thought pierced her heart like an arrow.

She had always loved him.

He turned now, searching the faces of the people gathered around until he found the one he was looking for.

"What were you thinking?" he shouted angrily, at Mary. "You know what happened to her. She has every right to be fearful! How could you be so callous?"

Mary pouted. "I was only trying to help," she sulked. "I thought she might get over her fear if I pushed her a little."

"You know nothing," he spat at her.

Mary turned and walked away.

The rest of the group slowly followed her, after assuring themselves that Lizzie was alright. Only Elam and Gloria remained.

"Are you okay?" Gloria was stroking her friend's arm. "I am so sorry, Lizzie! I didn't know she was going to do that."

Lizzie smiled weakly. "I am alright," she answered. Her voice sounded hoarse. "I just had a shock, that's all." She struggled to sit up, trying to reassure her friend.

"I should go back to the camp," she whispered. She looked at Elam, who sat next to her.

"I don't want to put anyone out, but would you be able to take me home?"

Elam looked sad. "If that's what you want, Lizzie," he answered.

"It is," she said. She stood up, not looking at him.

He looked like he was going to say something else, then changed his mind.

The three of them slowly started walking.

Lizzie didn't glance back at the lake, shimmering in the sun.

***

The plains and hills looked like they had been burnt golden by the sun, thought Lizzie as she meandered down the lane.

She had taken care with her appearance. She was wearing her best pale blue summer dress, with a crisp white *kapps* on her head. She had even condescended to put on a pair of shoes – she, who liked nothing better than walking barefoot on the earth so that she could feel the grass between her toes.

She didn't know why she felt the need to be neat. It wasn't as if it really mattered. But she had felt it, and so she did.

It was three weeks since the disastrous camping trip.

Lizzie had refused to speak of what had happened to her parents, retreating to her room. At first, she had been angry – angry at Mary for forcing her into the water, angry at herself for being so silly, angry at

God for taking her little brother. She had pounded her pillow with her fists, full of rage at life.

Then Elam's face had appeared before her.

She remembered him standing over her, dark against the sun, after he had rescued her. His eyes full of concern. The love for him that had flowed through her like nectar.

Love. It was the answer.

It didn't matter that Elam had dropped her home without barely speaking another word to her, and she had not seen him since. She knew she had no right to hope that his feelings for her might be the same as her own. It was enough that she saw his kindness and concern; it was enough that she felt love.

It was as if being in love had released her, somehow. The anger started to drain away. She felt something start to shift inside of her.

She could see the hill in the distance. Her heart started beating in an uncomfortable rhythm. She glanced down at the posy of wildflowers in her hand, picked along the way, as a gift.

She was almost there. And now her feet started dragging, an almost physical resistance. The identical markers stood silently in the ground, like sentinels of the earth.

She had never visited here, not since the day they had laid him to rest.

She could still vividly recall the dress she had worn – black, pressed and ironed perfectly. It had itched against her skin, making her scratch as she had stood here watching them lower him into the ground.

I'm sorry, Stephen. I'm sorry I couldn't protect you. I'm sorry I let you go.

There. She had arrived at his marker. It was plain, in keeping with their customs. It merely stated his name and age. A dragonfly hovered above it, before finally coming to rest on its edge. Lizzie stared at it. She couldn't help thinking it was a sign.

She saw him running around the yard, his blonde hair shining in the sun. He would curl up in her lap before bed, and she would always read him a story. He would wake in the night, sometimes, and she would be there, stroking his little head.

The tears when they came burst forth like a dam wall had fallen. She stood, sobbing, with her posy of wildflowers hanging in her hands.

It felt good to cry. She had kept it bottled inside for so long. It had become like a sore, festering and infecting her whole life.

It was because of Elam that she could finally acknowledge it; something in the way he had treated her, as if she wasn't an outcast meant to wonder the earth alone. It had broken something inside. He was a kindred spirit, she knew that now. It was like even the short amount of contact she had had with him at the lake had started the healing process in her.

She knew she had to let go.

And the peace of God, which surpasses all understanding, will guard your hearts and your minds in Jesus Christ.

The quote from Philippians 4:7 filled her mind. It was as if God had spoken directly to her, exactly when she needed Him to. For years, she had prayed and prayed, seeking peace which she had only found while walking the earth barefoot.

Her tears started drying. She knew it was okay. She could feel the presence of God all around her; she could clearly see her little brother sitting with Jesus, safe. In a garden, with the creatures of the earth surrounding him.

Thank you, Lord.

She placed the flowers on the grave, then turned and walked away.

She had only got to the end of the track when she saw a figure in the distance, resting against a buggy. She put her hand above her eyes to shield them from the sun. Who was it?

Her feet slowed. It couldn't be him. Could it?

Elam started walking toward her. He was dressed in his work clothes of shirt, pants and braces. A black hat shielded his blonde hair from the sun. A smile spread over his features.

"Your mother told me you were coming here," he said.

She approached him slowly. "I didn't think I would see you again," she stated simply.

"I wanted to give you some space," he answered. "After what happened at the lake." He looked around. "Walk with me?"

She nodded, slowly.

They meandered in companionable silence for a while.

"Lizzie." He stopped suddenly, turning to her. "I must speak with you." He took off his hat, twirling it nervously in his hands.

She turned to him. Why was he so beautiful to her? A lump formed in her throat just watching him.

"I must tell you all that is in my heart," he blurted.

She gasped. Was it possible?

He took her hand, turning her toward him.

"I love you, Lizzie," he breathed. "I think I have loved you for a long time. Spending time with you at the lake, it made me realise...." He stopped, struggling for words. "It made me realise what must have been in my heart all along."

She felt tears prick behind her eyes. "Oh, Elam! I never dreamed it would be possible. I have loved you, too, all along."

He grabbed her, hugging her fiercely. She felt as if she might burst with happiness.

"I think I knew after what Mary did to you," he said, into her hair. "I was so scared that I was going to lose you! I could see you struggling so badly in the water." He shuddered at the memory.

She put a hand to his face, caressing it gently. "But you saved me," she said. "You have saved me in more ways than that one, Elam." She took a deep breath. "That is why I could come here today, after all these years. Being with you made me realise that I must look forward in my life, not back."

"It has been so hard for you, my *lieb*," he said. "I remember all those years ago, when you came back to school after it happened. You were so lost and sad. I always wanted to say something to you to try to make it better, but I never had the words."

"You did make it better," she whispered. "Your kindness to me that day on the field showed me there was still goodness in the world. I felt such a failure, at everything, but you encouraged me. I had a crush on you after that, you know." She looked up at him, coloring slightly.

He grinned. "You were my crush, too! I think I recognized that we were alike – two birds of a feather."

She laughed.

He tilted her face slightly, staring down into her eyes. The moment stretched on, as he lowered his head and slowly kissed her.

She felt like she was in a dream, where time warped around itself. His lips were like coming home.

He took a deep breath. "Will you stay with me, forever? Two oddballs, side by side?"

Tears slipped down her cheeks. "It sounds like heaven," she whispered.

***

They parked the buggy and climbed down.

"Are you ready?" he asked gently.

She took a deep breath, then nodded.

He took her by the hand, leading her tenderly.

The water was cool; she gasped as they waded in.

For a moment, the old fear twisted inside of her.

Then she saw him, and felt his strong hand on hers, gripping her. She knew that he would never let go.

The water enveloped her, just like his arms. They stayed that way for what seemed like an eternity, watching the sun set over the lake. Streams of orange and pink hit the water, melding with the blue.

"All good?" he whispered.

"All good," she whispered back. And it was.

They waded back to the bank, dripping.

She glanced back, only for a moment. But in that time, she could clearly see her little brother, held in the hands of God for eternity.